"Why did you come here?"

"Would you believe nostalgia got the better of me? This is where we first met, Sally. We fell in love here. I kissed you for the first time next to the lockers right outside this room. You had blue paint on the end of your nose."

"I'm surprised you remember," she said, warmth stealing through her and blasting her reservations into oblivion.

"I remember everything about that time. Nothing I've known since has ever compared to it."

The warmth turned to melting heat. Against her better judgment she found herself wanting to believe him. "You don't have to say that. You *shouldn't* say it."

CATHERINE SPENCER, once an English teacher, fell into writing through eavesdropping on a conversation about Harlequin® romances. Within two months she had changed careers, and she sold her first book to Harlequin Presents® in 1984. She moved to Canada from England thirty years ago and lives in Vancouver. She is married to a Canadian and has four grown children—two daughters and two sons—plus a dog and a cat. In her spare time she plays the piano, collects antiques and grows tropical shrubs.

PASSION IN SECRET

CATHERINE SPENCER

MISTRESS MATERIAL

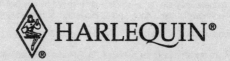

TORONTO • NEW YORK • LONDON
AMSTERDAM • PARIS • SYDNEY • HAMBURG
STOCKHOLM • ATHENS • TOKYO • MILAN • MADRID
PRAGUE • WARSAW • BUDAPEST • AUCKLAND

ISBN 0-373-80622-1

PASSION IN SECRET

First North American Publication 2004.

www.eHarlequin.com

Printed in U.S.A.

CHAPTER ONE

EVEN without the bitter wind howling in from the Atlantic, the hostile glances directed at her as she joined the other mourners at the graveside were enough to chill Sally to the bone. Not that anyone said anything. The well-bred residents of Bayview Heights, Eastridge Bay's most prestigious neighborhood, would have considered it sacrilege to voice their disapproval openly, before the body of one the town's most socially prominent daughters had been properly laid to rest.

No, they'd save their recriminations for later, over tea, sherry and sympathy at the Burton mansion. Except that Sally wouldn't be there to hear them. The blatant omission of her name from the list of guests invited to celebrate a life cut tragically short, was an indictment in itself, and never mind that her name had been officially cleared of blame.

"Earth to earth, ashes to ashes, dust to dust...." The minister, his robes flapping around him, intoned the final burial prayers.

Penelope's mother, Colette, gave a stifled sob and reached out to the flower-draped casket. Watching from beneath lowered lashes, Sally saw Fletcher Burton clasp his wife's arm in mute comfort. Flanking her other side and leaning heavily on his cane, Jake stood with his head bowed. His hair, though prematurely flecked with a hint of silver, was as thick as when Sally had last touched it, eight years before.

Seeming to sense he was being observed, he suddenly glanced up and caught her covert scrutiny. For all that she knew she was encouraging further censure from those busy watching *her,* she couldn't tear her gaze away. Even worse, she found herself telegraphing a message.

It wasn't my fault, Jake!

But even if he understood what she was trying to convey, he clearly didn't believe her. Like everyone else, he held her responsible. He was a widower at twenty-eight, and all because of her. She could see the condemnation in his summer-blue eyes, coated now with the same frost which touched his hair; in the unyielding line of his mouth which, once, had kissed her with all the heat and raging urgency perhaps only a nineteen-year-old could know.

A gust of wind tossed the bare, black boughs of the elm trees and caused the ribbon attached to the Burtons' elaborate wreath to flutter up from the casket, as if Penelope were trying to push open the lid from within. Which, if she could have, she'd have done. And laughed in the face of so much funereal solemnity.

Life's a merry-go-round, she'd always claimed, *and I intend to ride it to the end, and be a good-looking corpse!*

Remembering the words and the careless laugh which had accompanied them, Sally wondered if the stinging cold caused her eyes to glaze with tears or if, at last, the curious flattening of emotion which had held her captive ever since the accident, was finally releasing its unholy grip and allowing her to feel again.

A blurred ripple of movement caught her attention. Wiping a gloved hand across her eyes, she saw that the service was over. Colette Burton pressed her fingertips first to her lips and then to the edge of the casket in a last farewell. Other mourners followed suit—all except the widower and his immediate family. He remained immobile, his face unreadable, his shoulders squared beneath his navy pilot's uniform. His relatives closed ranks around him, as if by doing so, they could shield him from the enormity of his loss.

Averting her gaze, Sally stepped aside as, openly shunning her, Penelope's parents trekked over the frozen ground to the fleet of limousines waiting at the curb. She had attended the funeral out of respect for a former friend and because she knew her absence would fuel the gossip mills even more than her presence had. But the Burtons' message set the tone for the rest of the mourners following close behind: Sally Winslow was trouble, just as she'd always been, and undeserving of compassion or courtesy.

That being so obviously the case, she was shocked to hear footsteps crunching unevenly over the snow to where she stood, and Jake's voice at her ear saying, "I was hoping you'd be here. How are you holding up, Sally?"

"About as well as can be expected," she said, her breath catching in her throat. "And you?"

He shrugged. "The same. Are you coming back to the Burtons' for the reception?"

"No. I'm not invited."

He regarded her soberly a moment. "You are now. As Penelope's husband, I'm inviting you. Your friendship with her goes back a long way. She'd want you there."

She couldn't look at him. Couldn't bear the cool neutrality in his voice. "I'm not sure that's so," she said, turning away. "Our lives had gone in separate directions. We didn't always see eye to eye anymore." *Especially not about you or the sanctity of your marriage.*

Unmindful of the buzz of speculation such a gesture would surely give rise to, he gripped her arm to prevent her leaving. "It would mean a lot to me if you'd change your mind."

"Why, Jake?" she felt bound to ask. "You and I haven't been close in years, either, and under the circumstances, I can't imagine why you'd want to seek me out now."

"You were the last person to see my wife alive. The last one to speak to her. I'd like to talk to you about it."

"Why?" she said again, stifling a moment of panic. "The police report spells out the events of that night pretty clearly."

"I've read the police report and also heard my in-laws' account of what took place. It's what you have to say that interests me. *They* know that an accident occurred, but you're the only one who knows how or why."

The panic stole over her again. "I've already told everything there is to tell, at least a dozen times."

"Humor me, Sally, and tell it once more." He indicated the cane in his left hand. "They released me from the military hospital in Germany less than twenty-four hours ago. I got home early this morning, just in time for the funeral. Everything I've learned so far has come to me secondhand. Surely you can understand why I'd like to hear it from the only person who was actually there when Penelope died."

"What do you expect to accomplish by doing that?"

"It's possible you might remember something that didn't seem important at the time that you gave your statement. Something which would fill in what strike me as gaping holes in the accounts I've so far received."

In other words, he suspected there was more to the story than the nicely laundered official version. She'd been afraid of that. Afraid not of what he might ask, but that he'd discern the painful truth behind the lies she'd told to spare his and the Burtons' feelings.

"Sally?" Margaret, her older sister, bore down on them, her slight frown the only indication that she found Sally's fraternizing with the widower, in full sight of the bereaved family, to be totally inappropriate. "We need to leave. Now."

"Yes." For once glad of her older sister's interference, Sally put a respectable distance between herself and Jake.

"I was just explaining that I can't make it to the reception."

"Well, of course you can't!" Margaret's expression softened as she turned to Jake. "I'm very sorry about your loss, Jake, as are we all. What a dreadful homecoming for you. But I'm afraid we really do have to go. I need to get home to the children."

"You and Sally came here together?"

"Yes. She hasn't been too keen on driving since the accident. It shook her up more than most people seem to realize."

"Did it?" His glance swung from Margaret and zeroed in again on Sally with altogether too much perception for her peace of mind. "At least, you escaped serious injury."

"I was lucky."

"Indeed you were. A great deal more than my wife."

A trembling cold took hold as memories washed over her: of the protesting scream of the brakes, the smell of burning rubber as the tires left tracks on the road. And most of all, of Penelope, flung out of the car and lying all broken in the ditch, mumbling with a spectral smile on her face, *Silly me. I fell off the merry-go-round before it stopped, Sal.*

With an effort, Sally shook off the painful recollection and, aware that Jake continued to scrutinize her, said, "Yes, I was lucky. But not all injuries appear on the outside. Watching a friend die isn't something a person easily gets over."

"Not as a rule."

Although polite enough on the surface, his words rang with such searing contempt that, ignoring her better judgment, she burst out, "Do you think I'm lying?"

"Are you?"

"Good grief, Jake, even allowing for your understandable heartache, that question is uncalled-for!" Margaret seldom approved of anything Sally did, but when it came to outside criticism, she was all mother hen protecting her young. "My sister was—*is!*—devastated by Penelope's death."

Something shifted in his expression. Not a softening, exactly, but a sort of resignation. "Yes," he said. "Of course she is. I apologize, Sally, for implying otherwise."

Sally nodded, but her sigh of relief was cut short when he continued, "And I'll be glad to arrange a ride home for you after the reception."

"Thank you, Jake, but no. I've already inconvenienced Margaret. I wouldn't dream of imposing on you as well, especially not today."

"You'd be doing me a favor. And if you're afraid—"

"Why should she be?" Margaret interjected sharply. "Penelope's death was ruled an accident."

"I'm aware of that, just as I'm equally aware that not everyone accepts the verdict at face value."

"Then perhaps you're right. Perhaps taking her to the reception isn't such a bad idea." Margaret pursed her lips in thought, then gave Sally an encouraging poke in the ribs. "Yes. Go with him after all, Sally. Face the lot of them and prove you've got nothing to be ashamed of."

Rendered speechless by Margaret's sudden about-face, Sally groped for an answer which would put a definitive end to the whole subject. She had enough to cope with; she wasn't up to dealing with the unwarranted antagonism she'd face by agreeing to Jake's request.

"No!" she finally spluttered. "I don't have to prove anything to anyone!"

But the only person paying the slightest attention was Jake. Having issued her decree, Margaret had cut a brisk path among the graves to that section of the road where she'd parked her car a discreet distance away from any other vehicles, and was already climbing behind the wheel.

"It would seem," Jake murmured, clamping his free hand around Sally's elbow before she bolted also, and steering her toward the sole remaining limousine, "that you have no choice but to prove it. Let's not keep the driver waiting. I can't speak for you, but I'm in no shape to hike the four miles back to my in-laws', especially not under these conditions." He glanced up at the leaden sky pressing coldly down on the treetops. "We're lucky the snow held off this long."

Thankfully the last car was empty except for a couple from out of town who didn't seem to know that the passenger accompanying Jake was the woman whom popular opinion held responsible for rendering him a widower. Grateful that they showed no inclination to talk beyond a subdued greeting, Sally huddled in the corner of the soft leather seat and welcomed the blast of heat fanning around her ankles.

She'd be facing another round of chilly displeasure soon enough. In the meantime, she might as well take comfort wherever she could find it.

Lovely Sally Winslow was lying through her teeth. It might have been years since he'd last seen her, but Jake remembered enough about her to know when she was covering up. The question buzzing through his sleep-deprived mind was, for what purpose?

She'd been formally cleared of blame in the accident. So why couldn't she look him straight in the eye? Why was she instead staring fixedly out of the window beside her so that all he could see of her was the back of her head and the dark, shining cap of her hair. What was with her sitting as far away from him as she could get, as if she feared grief might prompt him to grab her by the throat and try to choke the truth out of her?

The chauffeur drove sedately along the broad, tree-lined

avenues of Bayview Heights, turned onto The Crescent and past various stately homes sitting on five acre lots, then hung a left through the iron gates guarding the Burton property. Except for the gleam of lamplight shining from the main floor windows and casting a soft yellow glow over the snow piled up outside, the massive house, built nearly a hundred years before from blocks of granite hewn from the quarry just outside town, rose black and brooding in the early dusk.

The limo barely whispered to a stop under the porte-cochère before Morton, the butler, flung open the double front doors. At the sight of Sally climbing the steps, a flicker of surprise crossed his face. ''Ahem,'' he said, extending one arm as if to bar her entry.

''Miss Winslow is here as my guest,'' Jake informed him, taken aback at the surge of protectiveness he felt toward her. Whatever else she might not be, Sally had always been able to fend for herself. She hardly needed him playing knight errant.

With fastidious distaste, Morton relieved her of her coat. ''The family is receiving in the drawing room, Captain Harrington,'' he said. ''Shall I announce you?''

''No need. I know the way.'' Jake handed the manservant his cap, brushed a few snowflakes from his shoulders and cocked his head at Sally. ''Ready to face the fray?''

''As much as I'll ever be.''

He thought of offering her his arm, and decided she'd have to make do with his moral support. No point in rubbing salt into his in-laws' wounds. They were suffering enough.

The drawing room, a masterpiece of late nineteenth-century craftsmanship with its intricate moldings and ornately coffered ceiling, hummed with the low buzz of conversation. Every spare inch of surface on the highly polished furniture was filled with photographs of Penelope framed by huge, heavily scented flower arrangements.

Under the tall Arcadian windows overlooking the rear gardens, a table held an assortment of fancy sandwiches, hot canapés and French pastries. A fat woman whom he didn't recognize presided over the heirloom sterling tea service and priceless translucent china. At the other end of the room, a Chippendale desk served as a temporary bar with his father-in-law in charge. Colette, an empty brandy snifter at her elbow, perched on the edge of a silk-upholstered chair, accepting condolences.

Fletcher Burton saw him and Sally first. At six foot one—only an inch shorter than Jake himself—he stood taller than most of the rest grouped about the room. About to pour sherry for the weepy-eyed woman at his side, he thumped the heavy cut-glass decanter back on its silver tray and cut a swath through the crowd. "I don't know how this young woman managed to get past Morton—!"

"I brought her here, Fletcher."

"What the devil for?"

"She and Penelope had known each other from childhood. They were friends. Sally was the last person to see your daughter alive. I'd say that gives her as much right to be here as anyone."

"For God's sake, Jake! You know Colette's feelings on this. We're trying to put the past behind us."

"With altogether more speed than decency, if you ask me."

"Nevertheless, under the circumstances, I hardly think—"

"I agreed to your taking charge of all the funeral arrangements because I couldn't be here in time to handle them myself," Jake cut in. "But may I remind you, Fletcher, that although you were Penelope's parents, I was her husband. I believe that entitles me to invite whom I please to this reception honoring her memory."

"No, it doesn't. Not if it adds to anyone's grief." Sally, who'd been edging back toward the foyer, spoke up. "I came to pay my respects, Mr. Burton, and now that I have, I'll leave."

"Thank you." Poor old Fletcher, henpecked to within an inch of his life, cast an anxious glance across the room to where Colette held court. "Look, I don't mean to be offensive, but I'm afraid you're no longer welcome in our home, Sally. If my wife should see you, she'd—"

But the warning came too late. Colette *had* seen them and her outraged gasp had everyone looking her way. Handkerchief fluttering, she fairly flew across the room. "How dare you show your face in our home, Sally Winslow? Have you no sense of decency at all?"

"She came with me." Not only was he beginning to sound like a broken record, Jake was growing thoroughly tired of repeating the same old refrain. It was his own fault, though. He should have stood his ground and insisted on postponing the funeral until he could have taken over. A few more days wouldn't have made any difference to Penelope, but if he'd hosted her wake in the house they'd shared as a couple, he might have been able to circumvent the present scene.

"How could you do that, Jake?" Colette wailed, her baby blues swimming in tears. "How could you hurt me by desecrating Penelope's memory this way? I've suffered enough. I need some closure."

"We all do, Colette," he said gently, moved despite himself by her anguish. Colette Burton might be a diva of the first order, but she'd truly adored her daughter.

"And you expect to find it by bringing that woman here?" She let out a tortured sob. "What kind of son-in-law are you?"

Fletcher would have caved at that line of attack, but Jake wasn't about to. ''One trying to put back together the pieces of his life.''

''With the help of your wife's murderer?''

The shocked reaction brought on by that remark—because there wasn't a soul in the room who hadn't heard it, including his parents—bounced back from the walls in a throttling silence broken only by a faint whimper of despair from Sally.

Caught again in the urge to leap to her defense, he said, ''Perhaps you'd like to retract that accusation, Colette, before it lands you in more trouble than you're able to handle right now.''

''No!'' Sally overrode him, her voice thick with emotion barely held in check. ''Don't blame her.'' She turned to Colette, and touched her hand contritely. ''Please forgive me, Mrs. Burton. I shouldn't have come. I just wanted to tell you again how very sorry I am that Penelope's life ended so tragically. I truly feel your pain.''

Colette snatched her hand away as if she'd been singed by a naked flame. ''Do you really, Sally Winslow! Are you trying to tell me you've walked the floor every night since she was killed, wondering what that strange noise is and realizing it's the sound of your own heart breaking, over and over again?''

''No, but I've—''

''Of course you haven't! You're probably glad Penelope's dead, if truth be known, because you always resented her for being prettier and smarter than you. But now, you don't have to live in her shadow anymore, do you?''

''Colette, that's enough.'' Fletcher tried steering her away, to no effect.

''Leave me alone! I'm not finished with her yet.'' Like a wild thing, she flung him off and rounded on Sally again.

"Do you have any idea how it feels to see your child lying dead in her box? Do you know what it's like to finally fall asleep from sheer emotional exhaustion, and do so praying that you'll never wake up again? *Do you?*"

Sally, pale enough to begin with, blanched alarmingly and pressed her lips together to stop their trembling. Perspiration gleamed on her brow. Her eyes, normally dark as forest-green pools, turned almost black with distress.

"That's what you've done to me, Sally Winslow." Colette's voice rose shrilly. "I'll never know another moment's peace, and I hope you never do, either! I hope what you've done haunts you for the rest of your miserable days!"

Again, Fletcher moved to intervene. "Hush now, Colette, my darling. You're overwrought."

She'd also fortified herself with more than one brandy and was three sheets to the wind, Jake belatedly realized. Her breath was enough to knock a man over. But it was Sally who suddenly fell limply against him and, before he could catch her, crumpled to the floor at his feet.

Drowning out the chorus of shocked exclamations, Colette teetered in Fletcher's hold and shrieked, "I hope she's dead! It's what she deserves!"

"Sorry to disappoint you," Jake said, stooping to feel the pulse, strong and steady, below Sally's jaw. "I'm afraid she's only fainted." Then, although he shouldn't have, he couldn't help adding, "Probably too much hot air in here. Where can we put her until she comes to?"

"The library," Fletcher said, handing a sobbing Colette over to one of her hangers-on. "She can lie down in there."

"I'll take her, Jake." His father materialized at his side. "You'll never make it with that injured leg."

"I'll manage somehow," he muttered, wishing his parents hadn't had to witness the scene just past. There'd never been much love lost between his family and the Burtons, and he knew they'd be upset by Colette's attack on him.

"You don't always have to be the iron hero, you know. It's okay to lean on someone else once in a while."

"Can the advice for another time, Dad," he said, a lot more abruptly than the man deserved. But cripes, his leg *was* giving him hell, and that alone was enough to leave him a bit short on tact. "It's my fault Sally's here at all. The least I can do is finish what I started. If you want to help, get Mom out of here. She looks as if she's seen and heard enough."

Clamping down on the pain shooting up this thigh, he scooped Sally into his arms and made his way through the crowd, which parted like the Red Sea before Moses. There might be some there who felt sorry for her, but no one except possibly his relatives dared show it. Colette had cornered the market on any spare sympathy that might be floating around.

The library was a man's room. Paneled in oak, with big, comfortable leather chairs and a matching sofa flanking the wide fireplace, some very good paintings, a Turkish rug and enough books to keep a person reading well into the next century, it was Fletcher's haven; the place to which he retreated when things became too histrionic with the women in his household. Jake had joined him there many a time, to escape or to enjoy an after-dinner drink, and knew he kept a private supply of cognac stashed in the bureau bookcase next to the hearth.

Just as well. Sally needed something strong to bring the color back to her face. Come to that, he could use a stiff belt himself.

Depositing her on the couch, he covered her with a mo-hair lap rug draped over one of the chairs. She looked very young in repose; very vulnerable. Much the way she'd looked when they'd started dating during her high school sophomore year. He'd been a senior at the time, and so crazy in love with her that he hadn't been able to think straight.

Even as he watched, she stirred and, opening her eyes, regarded him with dazed suspicion. "What are you doing?"

"Looking at you," he said, using the back of the sofa for support and wondering how she'd respond if he told her she had the longest damned eyelashes he'd ever seen, and a mouth so delectable that he knew an indecent urge to lean down and kiss it.

Get a grip, Harrington! You've been a widower less than a week, and should be too swamped with memories of your wife to notice the way another woman's put together—even if the woman in question does happen to have been your first love.

Her glance shied away from him and darted around the room. "How did I wind up in here?"

"I carried you in, after you fainted."

"I fainted?" She covered her eyes with the back of one hand and groaned in horror. "In front of all those people?"

"It was the best thing you could have done," he said, limping to the bureau and taking out a three-quarter-full bottle of Courvoisier cognac and two snifters. "You up-staged Colette beautifully. Without you to lambaste, she was left speechless." He poured them each a healthy shot of the liquor and offered one to her. "This should put you back on your feet."

"I don't know about that," she said doubtfully. "I haven't eaten a thing today."

"I wondered what made you pass out."

"I haven't had much of an appetite at all since…the accident."

"Feel up to talking about that night?"

She sat up and pushed her hair away from her face. "I

don't know what else I can say that you haven't already heard.''

Cautiously lowering himself into the nearest chair, he knocked back half the contents of his glass and, as the warmth of the brandy penetrated the outer limits of his pain, said, ''You could try telling me what really happened, Sally.''

The shutters rolled down her face, cloaking her expression. ''What makes you so sure there's more to tell?''

''You and I were once close enough that we learned to read each other's minds pretty well. I always knew when you were trying to hide something from me, and I haven't forgotten the signs.''

She swirled her drink but did not, he noticed, taste it. Why was she being so cagey? Could it be that she was afraid the booze might loosen her tongue too much and she'd let something slip? ''That was a long time ago, Jake. We were just kids. People grow up and change.''

''No, they don't,'' he said flatly. ''They just become better at covering up. But although you might have fooled everyone else, *including the police,* you've never been able to fool me. There's more to this whole business than anyone else but you knows, and I'm asking you, for old times' sake, to tell me what it is.''

Just for a moment, she looked him straight in the eye and he thought she was going to come clean. But then the door opened and Fletcher appeared. ''I expect you might need this, Jake,'' he said, brandishing the cane. ''And I wondered if Sally felt well enough for one of the chauffeurs to drive her home, before the cars fill up with other people.''

Masking his annoyance at the interruption, Jake said, ''Can't it wait another five minutes? We're in the middle of something, Fletcher, if you don't mind.''

''No, we're not,'' Sally said, throwing off the blanket

and swinging her legs to the floor. "If you can spare a car, I'd be very grateful, Mr. Burton. I'm more than ready to leave."

Frustrated, Jake watched as she tottered to her feet and wove her way to the door. Short of resorting to physical force, there was nothing he could do to detain her. This time.

But he'd see to it there was a next time. And when it happened, he'd make damn good and sure she didn't escape him until he was satisfied he knew the precise circumstances which had finally freed him from the hell his marriage had become.

CHAPTER TWO

YOU'VE never been able to fool me, he'd said, but he couldn't be more wrong. She'd fooled Jake about something a lot more momentous than the events leading up to Penelope's untimely end. She was very good at keeping secrets, even those which had ripped her life apart, both literally and figuratively.

Guarding this latest would be easy, as long as she didn't let him slip past her guard. And the only way to avoid that was to avoid him. Because, in her case, the old adage *Out of sight, out of mind,* had never applied to Jake Harrington. Just the opposite. No matter how many miles or years had separated them, he'd never faded from her memory. If anything, distance had lent him enchantment, and seeing him again had done nothing to change all that. The magic continued to hold.

He looked older, of course—didn't they all?—but the added years sat well on him. The boy had become a man; the youthful good looks solidified into a tough masculine beauty. Broader across the shoulders, thicker through the chest, he cut an impressive figure, especially in his military uniform. A person had only to look at him to know he'd seen his share of trouble, of tragedy, and emerged stronger for it. It showed in his manner, in the authority of his bearing.

This was not a man to shy away from the truth or crumble in the face of adversity. And she supposed, thinking about it as she made her way along the crowded halls of Eastridge Academy on the following Monday morning, in that respect at least he wasn't so very different from the boy who'd stolen her heart, all those years ago, in this very same school. Even at eighteen, he'd possessed the kind of courage which was the true mark of a man.

Still, Sally couldn't imagine telling him about Penelope. Male pride was a strange phenomenon. It was one thing for a man to climb behind the controls of a fighter jet and risk life and limb chasing down an anonymous enemy. And quite another to confront betrayal of the worst kind from the woman he'd married, *especially* if he discovered he was the last to know about it.

The senior secretary called out to her as she passed through the main office on her way to the staff lounge. "Morning, Sally. You just missed a phone call."

"Oh? Any message."

"No. Said he'd try to catch you later on."

He? "Did he at least give a name?"

"No." The secretary eyed her coyly. "But he had a voice to die for! Dark and gravelly, as though he needed a long drink of water which I'd have been happy to supply. Sound like anyone you know?"

Premonition settled unpleasantly in the pit of Sally's stomach but she refused to give it credence. Plenty of men had dark, gravelly voices. That Jake could be numbered among them was pure coincidence. "Probably someone's father calling to complain I give too much homework. If he happens to phone back, try to get a number where he can be reached. I'm going to be tied up with students all day."

"Will do. Oh, and one more thing." The secretary nodded at the closed door to her left. "Mr. Bailey wants to see you in his office before classes start."

Oh, wonderful! A private session with the Academy principal who also happened to be her brother-in-law and definitely not one of her favorite people. The day was off to a roaring start!

"You asked to see me, Tom?"

Tom Bailey looked up from the letter he was reading, his brow furrowed with annoyance at the interruption of Very Important Administrative Business. "This isn't a family gathering, Ms. Winslow. If you're determined to ignore professional protocol, at least close the door before you open your mouth."

"Good morning to you, too." Without waiting to be invited, she took a seat across from him. "What's on your mind, *Mr. Bailey?*"

"Margaret tells me you managed to get yourself invited to the reception at the Burtons' on Saturday."

"I prefer to say I was coerced—as much by your wife as anyone else."

He leaned back in his fancy swivel chair and fixed her in his pale-eyed stare, the one he used to intimidate freshmen. "Regardless, let me remind you what I said when all this mess with Penelope Harrington started. Our school prides itself on its fine reputation and I won't tolerate its being sullied by scandal. Bad enough you've been on staff less than a month before your name's splashed all over the front pages of every newspaper within a fifty-mile radius, without any more shenanigans now that the fuss is finally beginning to die down. I did you a favor when I persuaded the Board of Governors to give you a position here, because—"

"Actually," Sally cut in, "I'm the one who did you a favor, Tommy, by stepping in at very short notice when my predecessor took early maternity leave and left you short one art teacher."

He turned a dull and dangerous shade of red. Subordinates did not interrupt the principal of the Academy and they particularly did not challenge the accuracy of his pronouncements. "You showed up in town unemployed!"

"I *came home* looking forward to a long-overdue vacation which I cut short because you were in a bind.'' She glanced pointedly at the clock on the wall. "Is there anything else, or am I free to go and do what the Board hired me to do? I have a senior art history class starting in ten minutes.''

If it hadn't been beneath his dignity, he'd have gnashed his perfectly flossed teeth. Instead he made do with a curt, "As long as we understand one another.''

"I've never had a problem understanding you, Tom,'' she said, heading for the door. "My sister's the one I can't figure out. I've never been able to fathom why she married you.''

As soon as the words were out of her mouth, she regretted them. She'd been known as a wild child in her youth, but she liked to think she'd matured into a better person since—one for whom taking such cheap shots wasn't her normal style. But "normal'' had been in short supply practically from the minute she'd set foot in town again, beginning with the morning she and Penelope Burton Harrington had happened to run into one another in the Town Square.

"Sally!'' Penelope had fairly screamed, rushing to embrace her as if a rift spanning nearly a decade had never crippled their friendship. "Oh, it's wonderful to see you again! It's been like living in a tomb around here lately, but now that you're back, it'll be just like old times, and we can kick some life into the place.''

The cruel irony of her words had come back to torment Sally during the long, sleepless nights since the accident. But thanks to Tom's having hired her, at least her days were too busy to allow for much wallowing in useless guilt, which made her parting remark to him all the more unforgivable. To satisfy her own sense of fair play, the least she could do was seek him out later and apologize.

She had a full teaching load that day, though, plus a

meeting at lunch with the nit-picking head of the Fine Arts department, and an after-school interview with a furious student who didn't understand why copying an essay on Henri Matisse from the Internet was plagiarism and warranted a big fat F on his midterm report.

Somehow, the events of first thing slipped to the back of her mind and she forgot about Tom. She forgot, too, about that morning's phone call from the man who hadn't left a message.

But he didn't forget about her. He came to her classroom just as she was stuffing her briefcase with the assignments she planned to mark that evening. By then it was after five o'clock and the building was pretty much deserted except for the cleaning staff. In fact, when she heard the door open, she was so sure it was the janitor, come to empty the waste bins and clean up the sinks, that she said, "I'll be out of your way in just a second," without bothering to look up from her task.

The door clicked closed which, in itself, should have alerted her to trouble. "No rush. I've got all the time in the world," came the reply, and there it was: the dark, gravelly voice which had so captivated the school secretary earlier.

It didn't captivate Sally. It sent shock waves skittering through her. The stack of papers in her hand flipped through her fingers and slithered over the floor. Flustered, she dropped to her knees and began gathering them together in an untidy bundle.

"I'd no idea teachers put in such long hours," Jake said, his cane thudding softly over the floor as he came toward her. "Let me help you pick those up."

"No, thank you!" Hearing the betraying edge of panic in her voice, she took a deep breath and continued more moderately, "I don't need your help. In fact, you shouldn't be here at all. If Tom Bailey finds out—"

"He won't. His was the only car in the parking lot and he was leaving as I arrived. We're quite alone, Sally. No one will disturb us."

She was afraid of that! "Oh, really? What about the cleaning staff?"

"They're busy in the gym and won't get down to this end of the building for at least another hour." His hand came down and covered hers as she scrabbled with the pages still slipping and sliding from her grasp. "You're shaking. Are you going to faint again?"

"Certainly not!" she said, scooting away from him before he realized how easily his touch scrambled her brains and stirred up memories best left untouched. "I just don't like people creeping up and taking me by surprise, that's all."

"I'm not 'people,' and I didn't creep." He tapped his bad leg. "It's a bit beyond my capabilities, these days."

"No, you're the wounded hero come home to bury his wife, but if you insist on being seen with me at every turn, you're going to lose the public outpouring of sympathy you're currently enjoying, and become as much of a pariah as I have."

"I'm not looking for sympathy, my lovely. I'm looking for information."

My lovely…that's what he'd called her in the days when they'd been in love; when they'd *made* love. And the sound of it, falling again from his lips after all this time, brought back such a shock of déjà vu that she trembled inside.

Late August, the summer she'd turned seventeen, just weeks before he started his junior year at university, two hundred miles away…wheeling gulls against a cloudless sky, the distant murmur of the incoming tide, the sun gilding her skin, and Jake sliding inside her, with the tall grass of the dunes whispering approval in the sea breeze. "I miss you so much when we're apart," he'd told her. *"I'll love you forever."*

But he hadn't. Thirteen months later, she'd spent two months studying art in France. When she returned, she found out from Penelope that he'd been seeing a college coed while she'd been gone.

She'd been crushed, although she really shouldn't have been. As her weeks abroad passed, there'd been signs enough that trouble was brewing. His phone calls had dwindled, become filled with long, awkward pauses. He wasn't there to meet her as promised, when she came home again. He didn't even make it back for Thanksgiving. And finally, when there was no avoiding her at Christmas, he'd shamelessly flaunted her replacement in her face.

"Jake Harrington's a two-timing creep," sweet sympathetic Penelope told her, *"and you're too smart to let such a worthless jerk break your heart. Forget him! There are better fish in the sea."*

But she hadn't wanted anyone else. As for forgetting, it was a lot easier said than done for an eighteen-year-old who'd just discovered she was pregnant by the boy she adored and who'd passed her over for someone new.

The spilled assignments at last cradled in her arms, Sally struggled to her feet with as much grace as she could muster and crammed the papers into her briefcase. "We went over all this on Saturday. I've told you everything there is to know."

"Okay." He shrugged amiably. "Then I won't ask you again."

Elation flooded through her. "I'm glad you finally believe me."

"Of course I do," he said. "You're not the kind of person who'd hold out on me about something this important, are you?"

Guilt and suspicion nibbled holes in her relief. "Then why did you come here to begin with?"

"Mostly to find out if you've forgiven me for landing you in such a mess an Saturday. If I'd known Colette was going to go after you like that—"

"You had no way of knowing she'd react so badly. Consider yourself forgiven."

"A lot of women wouldn't be so understanding," he said diffidently. "But then, you never were like most women."

Diffident? Jake Harrington?

She'd have laughed aloud at the idea, had it not been that the hair on the back of her neck vibrated with warning. He was up to something! She could almost hear the wheels spinning behind that guileless demeanor! "And?"

"Hmm?" Doing his best to look innocently virtuous, he traced a herringbone pattern over the floor with the tip of his cane.

"You said 'mostly'—that you were here *mostly* to find out if I'd forgiven you. What's the other reason?"

He tried to look sheepish. Would have blushed, if he'd had it in him to do such a thing. "Would you believe, nostalgia got the better of me? When I heard you were on staff here, I couldn't stay away." He leaned against one of the cabinets holding supplies and sent her a smile which plucked unmercifully at her heartstrings. "This is where we met, Sally. We fell in love here. I kissed you for the first time next to the lockers right outside this room. You had blue paint on the end of your nose."

"I'm surprised you remember," she said, warmth stealing through her and blasting her reservations into oblivion.

"I remember everything about that time. Nothing I've known since has ever compared to it."

The warmth turned to melting heat. Against her better judgment, she found herself wanting to believe him. "You don't have to say that. You *shouldn't* say it."

"Why not? Don't I have as much right to tell the truth as you do?"

He sounded so sincere, she found herself wondering. *Was* he playing mind games with her? Trying to trip her up? Or was she seeing entrapment where none existed?

Deciding it was better to err on the side of caution and put an end to the meeting, she indicated the bulging briefcase and said, "I should get going. I've got a full evening's work ahead."

He eased himself away from the desk. "Me, too. I'm still sorting through Penelope's stuff and deciding what to do with it, and the house. I don't need all that space."

Watching as he limped to the door, she knew an inexplicable regret that he accepted his dismissal so easily. So what if his smile left her insides fluttering? They weren't teenagers anymore. First love didn't survive an eight-year winter of neglect to bloom again at the first hint of spring.

Still, having him show up so unexpectedly had unsettled her almost as badly as seeing him at the funeral. He stirred up too many buried feelings.

His voice, the curve of his mouth, the latent passion in his direct blue gaze, made her hungry for things she shouldn't want and certainly couldn't have. So, rather than risk running into him again, she waited until his footsteps faded, and the clang of the outside door shutting behind him echoed down the hall, before she ventured out to retrieve her coat from the staff cloakroom.

The sky had been clear when she left for work that morning and she'd enjoyed the two-mile walk from the guest cottage at the end of her parents' driveway and through the park to the school. Sometime since classes ended, though, the clouds had rolled in again and freezing rain begun to fall. The ramp beyond the Academy's main entrance was treacherous with black ice.

Twice, she'd have lost her footing, had it not been for

the iron railing running parallel to the path. But the real trouble started when she gained the glassy sidewalk and found it impossible to navigate in shoes not designed for such conditions.

Turning right, as she intended to do, was out of the question. Instead, with her briefcase rapping bruisingly against her leg, she lurched into the dirty snow piled next to the curb, three days earlier, by the road-clearing crews.

It was the last straw in a day which had started badly and gone steadily downhill ever since. Exasperated, she gave vent to a stream of unladylike curses which rang up and down the deserted street with satisfying gusto.

Except the street wasn't quite as deserted as she'd thought. A low-slung black sports car, idling in the lee of a broad-trunked maple not ten feet away, cruised to a stop beside her, with the passenger window rolled down just far enough for Jake's voice to float out. "Faculty members didn't know words like that when I was a student here," he announced affably. "Come to think of it, I'm not sure I knew them, either."

"Are you stalking me?" she snapped, miserably conscious of the fact that she cut a ridiculous figure standing there, ankle-deep in snow.

"Not at all. I stopped to offer you a ride home."

"No, thanks. I prefer to walk."

"Oh," he said. "Is that what you were doing when you came sailing into the gutter just now?"

"I temporarily lost my balance."

"Temporarily?" He let out a muffled snort of laughter. "Dear Ms. Winslow, if you insist on wearing summer footwear in the kind of winter which Eastridge Bay is famous for, it'll be anything but temporary. Stop being stubborn and get in the car before you break your neck. I'd come round and hold the door open for you, except I'm having enough problems of my own trying to get around in these conditions.''

She debated telling him what he could do with his offer, but her frozen feet won out over her pride. ''Just as well you're not inclined to play the gentleman,'' she muttered, yanking open the door and climbing in to the blessed warmth of the car. ''I might be tempted to knock your cane out from under you!''

''Now that,'' he remarked, stepping gently on the gas and pulling smoothly out into the road, ''is why some people—people who don't know you as well as I used to—talk about you the way they do.''

''And how is that, exactly? I'm living in the guest cottage on my parents' estate, by the way. You turn left on—''

''I remember how to get there, Sally,'' he said. ''I've driven you home often enough, in the past. And to answer your question, unflatteringly. They say you came back to town and brought a bagful of trouble with you. Are they right?''

''Why ask me? You'll find listening to their version of the facts far more entertaining, I'm sure.''

''As a matter of interest, where *have* you been for the last several years?''

''At university on the West Coast, and after that, down in the Caribbean.''

He didn't quite snicker in her face, but he might as well have. ''Doing what?'' he inquired, his voice shimmering with amusement.

''Well, not weaving sun hats from coconut palm fronds or singing in a mariachi band, if that's what you're thinking!''

''You have no idea what I'm thinking, Sally. None at all. And you haven't answered my question. What kept you in the sunny Caribbean all this time?''

"The same thing that's keeping me occupied here. Teaching, except the children down there were so under-privileged that working with them was pure pleasure."

"Very commendable of you, I'm sure. How long did you stay?"

"Two years in Mexico, and two years on the island of St. Lucia after that."

"Why that part of the world?"

"They needed teachers as badly as I needed to get away from here."

"What?" His voice quivered with silent laughter. "You never yearned to settle down in picturesque Eastridge Bay? To follow in your sister's footsteps and marry a fine, up-standing man of good family?"

Once upon a time I did, but you chose to put a wedding ring on Penelope's finger, instead! "Not all women see marriage as the be-all and end-all of happiness. Some of us find satisfaction in a career."

"But not everyone runs away to a tropical island to find it."

"I was trying to escape the winters up here. But this town is my home and I was happy to come back to it—until everything started going wrong." She shivered inside her coat. The rain, she noticed, had turned to snow and was sliding down the windshield in big, sloppy flakes. She noticed, too, that they'd passed the turnoff for Bayview Heights blocks before, and were speeding instead along the main boulevard leading out of town. "You're going the wrong way, Jake!"

"So I am," he said cheerfully.

"Well, turn around and head back! And slow down while you're at it. I've spent enough time stuck in a snow-bank, for one night."

"No need to get all exercised, Sally. Since I've missed

the turn anyway, we might as well enjoy a little spin in the country.''

''I don't want to go for a spin in the country,'' she told him emphatically. ''I want to go home.''

''And you will, my lovely. All in good time.''

''Right now!'' She reached for the door handle. ''Stop this car at once, Jake Harrington. And stop calling me that.''

He didn't bother to reply. The only sound to register above the low hum of the heater was the click of automatic door locks sliding home and the increased hiss of the tires on the slick surface of the road.

Stunned, she turned to stare at him. There were no streetlights this far beyond the town limits, but the gleam of the dashboard lights showed his profile in grim relief. ''Are you kidnapping me?''

''Don't be ridiculous.''

''Then just what *are* you doing?''

''Looking for a place where we can get something hot to drink. It's the least I can do, to make up for keeping you out past your bedtime.''

The words themselves might have been innocuous enough, but there was nothing affable or benign in his tone of voice. The man who'd beguiled her with his smile and tender memories not half an hour ago, who'd offered her a ride home to spare her walking along icy streets, had turned into a stranger as cold and threatening as the night outside.

''You had this planned all along, didn't you?'' she said, struggling to suppress the fear suddenly tapping along the fringes of her mind. She'd accepted a lift from her one-time lover, the local hero come home from doing battle and with the scars to prove it, not from some faceless stranger, for heaven's sake! To suspect he posed any sort of threat was nothing short of absurd. ''This is what you intended, from the minute you showed up in my classroom.''

"Yes," he said.

"Well, you didn't have to go to such extremes. I'd have been happy to stop for coffee at a place in town."

"Too risky. Think of the gossip, if we'd been seen together. The widower and the wild woman flaunting their association in public! Better to find some out-of-the-way place where the kind of people we know wouldn't dream of setting foot. A place so seedy, no respectable woman would want to be seen by anyone she knew."

Seedy? What on earth would prompt him to use such a word?

Numbly she stared ahead, once again in the grip of that eerie unease. By then, the snow had begun to settle, turning the windows opaque except for the half-moons cleared by the windshield wipers. She could see nothing of the landscape flying past, nothing of where they'd been or where they were headed.

Then, off to the side, some hundred yards or so down the road, a band of orange light pierced the gloom; a neon sign at first flashing dimly through the swirling snow, but growing brighter as the car drew nearer, until there was no mistaking its message. Harlan's Roadhouse it read. Beer— Eats—Billiards.

And her premonition crystalized into outright dismay. She'd seen that sign before. And Jake was well aware of the fact!

He slowed to turn into the rutted parking area, nosed the car to a spot close to the tavern entrance and turned off the engine. Immediately the muffled, relentless throb of country and western music filled the otherwise quiet night, its only competition the equally brutal pounding of Sally's heart.

He climbed out of the car and, despite his earlier claim that he was too lame to play the gentleman, came around and opened the passenger door. When she made no move to join him, he reached across to unclip her seat belt and grasped her elbow. "This is as far as we go, Sally," he said blandly. "Hop out and be quick about it."

"I'd rather not."

"I'd rather you did. And I'm not taking you back to town until you do."

Odd how a man's mood could shift so abruptly from mild to menacing; how smoldering rage could make its presence felt without a voice being raised. And stranger still that a person could find herself responding hypnotically to a command she knew would result in nothing but disaster.

Like a sleepwalker, she stepped out into the snow, yet felt nothing of its stinging cold. Was barely aware of putting one foot in front of another as she walked beside Jake, past the rusted pickup trucks and jalopies, to the entrance of the building.

"After you," he said, pushing open the scarred wooden door and ushering her unceremoniously into the smoke-filled interior.

At once, the noise blasted out to meet her. The smell of beer and cheap perfume, mingled with sweat and tobacco, assailed her senses.

Stomach heaving, she turned to Jake. "Please don't make me do this!"

"Why ever not?" he asked, surveying her coldly. "Place not to your liking?"

"No, it's not," she managed to say. "I'm insulted you'd even ask."

"But it was good enough the night you came here with Penelope, the night she died, wasn't it?" he said. "So why not now, with me?"

CHAPTER THREE

SHE didn't reply, nor had he expected she would. He'd outmaneuvered her too thoroughly. Instead she hovered just inside the door, uncertain whether to flee or surrender. Since he hadn't a hope in hell of catching her if she tried to make a run for it, he eliminated the possibility by marching her to a booth on the other side of the dance floor.

"Cosy, don't you think?" he said, sliding next to her on the shabby vinyl banquette so that she was trapped between him and the wall. Too bad he had to put his mouth to her ear for her to hear him. He didn't need the dizzying scent of her hair and skin making inroads on his determination to wring the truth out of her.

"What'll it be, folks?" A giant of a man, with beefy arms covered in tattoos and a head as bald as an egg, came out from behind the bar and swiped a dirty cloth over the tabletop.

Without bothering to consult her, Jake said, "Beer. Whatever you've got on tap. And nachos."

"I don't drink beer and I don't like nachos," she said snootily, the minute the guy left to fill their order.

"No?" Jake dug in his hip pocket for his wallet. "What did you have the last time you were here—champagne and oysters on the half shell?"

"What makes you think I've been here before?"

"I read the police report, remember?"

She slumped against the wall, defeated. "Why are you doing this, Jake?" she asked, raising her voice over the din from the jukebox. "What do you hope to accomplish?"

"I want to know why my wife made a habit of frequenting places like this while I was away on combat duty, and if *you* won't tell me, I'll find someone here who will."

"You're wasting your time. Penelope and I were here only once, and when I realized the kind of place it was, I insisted we leave."

He scanned the room at large. On the other side of the dance floor, a woman much the worse for wear had climbed on a table and was gyrating lewdly to the applause of the patrons lining the bar. Swinging his gaze to Sally again, Jake asked, "Was it your idea to stop here to begin with?"

"Certainly not!" she snapped. Then, realizing how much she'd revealed with her indignation, added, "We'd decided to drive out to a country inn for dinner that night, it started snowing on the way home, the roads were even worse than they are tonight, and we were looking for a place to wait out the storm. Why is that so hard for you to believe?"

"It's not, Sally. But nor does it explain what made you change your minds and venture back on the road anyway, before the weather improved. One look out the door, and you must have known you were taking your lives in your hands by getting back behind the wheel of a car."

"I already told you. We didn't like the...clientele here."

The tattooed hulk returned just then. "Where's your gal pal tonight?" he asked, sliding a tankard of beer across the table to Sally. "The regulars miss seein' her around the joint. She knew how to party."

"You know what they say," Jake cut in, before Sally could answer, even assuming she could come up with anything plausible after having just been exposed as a blatant liar. "Three's a crowd."

The server's face split in a grin. He had a scar running down one side of his massive neck and was missing three front teeth. Probably got the first from a knife wound, and lost the rest in a brawl. "Little old Penny-wise wouldn't horn in on your date for long, dude. Plenty of guys around here'd be only too willing to take her off your hands.''

''I think,'' Sally said, in a small, despairing voice, as the oaf lumbered off to collect their nachos, ''I'm going to be sick.''

Unmoved, Jake knocked back half his beer. ''That tends to happen when a person's attempt to hide the truth blows up in her face. I'd bet my last dollar you'd feel a whole lot better if you'd spit out the load of rubbish you've been feeding me.''

''It would serve you right if I did!'' she cried with surprising passion. ''But since truth's so all-fired important to you, try this on for size—I don't know what happened to turn the boy I used to know into such a hard-nosed bully, but I do know I don't like the man you've become.''

He didn't much like it himself. Browbeating a woman—*any woman*—wasn't his style. Traumatizing Sally to the point that she looked as bewildered as an innocent victim caught in enemy crossfire filled him with self-loathing. He hadn't come home to continue the inhumane practices of war. He'd come looking for a little peace.

Trouble was, he was no closer to finding it here than he had been on the other side of the world, and it was eating him alive, though not for the reasons Sally might suppose.

Hardening his heart against her obvious distress, he said, ''I'm not especially enamored of you, either. I'd hoped by now that you'd outgrown the habit of taking the easy way out of whatever tight spot you happen to find yourself in.''

She picked up her tankard of beer and, for a second, he thought she might fling it in his face. But at the last minute, she shoved it away and spat, ''I resent that, and I refuse to sink to the level of the company in which I find myself. I might be all kinds of things, but I've never lied to you in the past.''

"*Never,* Sally? Not once? Not even to spare my feelings?"

She opened her mouth to reply, but at the last minute appeared to think better of it. Her eyes grew huge and haunted, and filled with tears.

He wanted to wipe them away. Wanted to take her in his arms and tell her he was sorry; that raking up the distant past wasn't his intent because it didn't matter—not any of it. He wanted to tell her that he could forgive her anything, if only she'd free him to live in the present and be able to face the future without guilt weighing him down and souring each new day. And the depth of his wanting staggered him.

His wife was barely cold in her grave, for Pete's sake, and all his suspicions aside, common decency demanded he at least observe a token period of mourning.

Slamming the door on thoughts he couldn't afford to entertain, he drained his beer. "I don't know who it is you think you're protecting, Sally," he said, "but to prove I'm not completely heartless, I'll make a deal with you. Instead of badgering you to betray secrets you obviously hold sacred, I'll spell out what I believe happened, the night Penelope died. All I ask of you is that you tell me honestly whether or not I'm on the right track. Agree to those terms and, after tonight, I'll never bring the subject up again."

She moistened her lips with the tip of her tongue and stared stubbornly at her hands, but he could see she was wavering.

"I'll give you some time to think about it," he offered, levering himself away from the table and grabbing his cane, "but don't take too long. I'll only be gone a few minutes."

He wove his way through the couples squirming up against each other on the dance floor, knowing she was watching him the entire time. The men's room lay at the end of a long, badly lit corridor toward the rear of the building. A boy no more than eighteen swayed in the doorway, vacant-eyed and decidedly green about the gills. The squalor in the area beyond defied description.

Cripes! Jake had known his share of dives, but this one took some beating!

"Hey, pal," he said, catching the kid just in time to stop him doing a face plant on the filthy floor, and propelling him toward the back exit. "How about a breath of fresh air?"

The snow had tapered off, and a few stars pricked the sky. A clump of pines bordering the parking lot glowed ghostly white in the dark. Somewhere across the open fields to the west, a pack of coyotes on the hunt howled in unison. Under different circumstances, it would have been a magical night, peaceful and quiet, except for nature's music.

Propping the boy against the wall, Jake rubbed a handful of snow in his face. The poor guy gasped and shuddered. Doubled over. Recognizing the inevitable was about to occur, Jake stood well to one side.

"Feel better?" he asked, when the kid finally stopped retching.

"I guess."

"What's your name?"

He wiped the back of his hand across his mouth. "Eric."

"You of legal age to be hanging around bars, Eric?"

"No," he moaned miserably, sagging against the wall.

"Didn't think so. You live far from here?"

"Down the road some." He swallowed and grimaced. "A mile, maybe."

Jake weighed the options. He had problems enough of his own, without taking on someone else's. And a mile was no distance at all. The kid was young and strong; he could walk it in a quarter of an hour. Less, if he put his mind to it and didn't get sidetracked by the next bar he passed along the way.

But the temperature had dropped well below freezing, and he wasn't in the best shape. Jake's playing Good Samaritan would take all of five minutes. He could be back before Sally had the chance to miss him.

More important, he'd be able to sleep that night with a clear conscience. He'd been young and stupid himself, at one time, and felt for the poor kid whose troubles had only just begun. By morning, he'd be nursing one mother of a hangover!

He zipped up his jacket and fished the car keys out of his pocket. "Come on," he said. "I'll drive you."

"That's okay. I can walk."

"You can barely stand, you damn fool!"

The kid started to cry. "I don't want my mom to see me fallin'-down drunk. She's not gonna like it."

"If you were my son, I wouldn't like it, either." He jerked his thumb over his shoulder at the building behind. "But I'll bet money she'd rather have you passing out at home, than winding up as roadkill when that lot in there decide to hit the highway."

If she hadn't been so preoccupied, she might have noticed the man sooner. But by the time she realized she'd become the object of his attention, he'd lurched onto the bench beside her and slung a sweaty arm around her shoulders. "Lookin' for company, babe?"

"No," she said, recoiling from the foul breath wafting in her face. "I'm with someone."

He made a big production of swinging his head to the left and right, and then, with a drunken guffaw, peering under the table. "Don't look that way to me," he snickered, lifting his smelly T-shirt to scratch at the hairy expanse of blubber underneath. "Looks to me like you're all on your little ol' lonesome, and just waitin' for Sid to show you a good time."

"No, really! I'm with...my boyfriend. He's just gone...." *Where,* exactly, that it was taking him so long?

"To take a leak?" Sid chortled and reached for her untouched beer.

Good grief, could the clientele possibly have sunk even lower than the last time she'd set foot in this place? Revolted, she shrank into the corner of the booth, as far away from him as she could get, and made no effort to disguise her abhorrence.

Big mistake! Sid's eyes, close-set and mean enough to begin with, narrowed menacingly. He slid nearer, pressed his thigh against hers. "Wha'samatter, honey? Think you're too good for a stud like me?"

"Not at all," she said, averting her face. "I'm sure you're a very nice man."

"Better believe it, babe." His hand clamped around her chin, and forced her to turn and look at him again. He shoved his face closer, licked his lips. The fingers of his other hand covered her knee. Began inching her skirt up her leg. "Better be real friendly with Sid, if you know what's good for you."

Oh, God! Where was Jake?

Sid's fingers slid under the hem of her skirt. Crawled over her knee. Someone plugged another selection in the juke box: Patsy Cline singing "Crazy."

How appropriate! Unable to help herself, Sally giggled hysterically.

Sid squeezed her thigh. "Tha's better, babe! Treat me right, and I'll make you feel *real* good."

By then, so unnerved that she could barely breathe, she seized on the first escape possibility that occurred to her. "Dance with me," she said, praying he wouldn't hear the terror crowding her voice. Praying that he was too clumsily drunk to realize until it was too late that the only thing she wanted was to get out of the confining booth and put some distance between him and her.

"Sure thing, babe!" He grinned evilly and, with bone-crushing strength, hauled her bodily off the seat and into his arms, and pinned her like a butterfly against him.

At least, though, his hand was no longer creeping up her thigh! At least she stood a better chance of distracting him long enough to wriggle free. And if that didn't work, she could scream for help and stand a reasonable chance of being heard by the other bodies crammed on the dance floor.

"Start enjoyin', babe," Sid grated. "Ain't no fun dancin' with a corpse."

If he'd left it at that, she might have survived unscathed. But as added inducement, he stuck his tongue in her ear. Repelled beyond endurance and unmindful of the consequences of her action, she responded by lifting her knee and ramming it full force in his groin at the same time that she raked her fingernails down his face.

He roared like a wounded bear, reared back and landed a vicious slap to the side of her head. The grimy silver ball rotating from the ceiling swung crazily in her line of vision. The faces of the people around her tilted; their voices merged with coarse laughter into a cacophony of unintelligible sound.

Dazed, she lifted her head and saw his fist coming at her again. Pain cracked against her cheek in a burst of fire. She crumbled to her hands and knees on the filthy floor. Tasted blood, warm and salty on her tongue. Felt him grab her by the hair. Savagely yank her to her feet again.

Then, as suddenly as he'd latched on to her, he backed away, felled by a blow from behind. Jake, his face a distorted mask of white fury, his eyes blazing, swam into view.

A woman nearby screamed, someone else swore. Needing no better excuse to start a fight, half the men in the room joined in the fray, indiscriminately landing punches on whoever happened to be handy. But they gave Jake a wide berth. Drunken hoodlums though they might be, they had no wish to tangle with a man wielding a cane like a shillelagh and clearly willing to crack the skull of anyone foolish enough to challenge him.

Weaving his way to her through the pandemonium, he reached an arm around her waist and pulled her against him. Up to that point, she'd been too focused on defending herself to give in to the terror screaming along her nerves. Surviving the moment had been the only thing of import. But at his touch, at the cold, clean scent of him and the solid reassurance of his body shielding hers, she fell apart completely.

"I thought he was going to kill me!" she sobbed, burying her face against his neck.

He stroked her hair, murmured her name, and oh, it felt so good to be held by him again. So good to hear the old tenderness creep into his voice. Despite all the chaos and din pulsing around them, he created a tiny haven of safety she never wanted to leave.

He was of a more practical turn of mind. "Let's get out of here while we still can," he muttered, hustling her toward the door. "Things are going to get uglier before the night's over."

Just as they reached it, though, the door flew open and half a dozen police burst into the room, making escape impossible. "Hold it right there. Nobody leaves until I say so," the officer leading the pack ordered, and even in her shocked state, Sally recognized him as one of those who'd been first on the scene, the night Penelope had died.

He recognized her, too, which was hardly surprising, given the amount of publicity the accident had received in the local news. "Not you again!" he said, on an exasperated breath, as his colleagues set about restoring order. "Gee, lady, how many times does it take before you learn your lesson and stay away from places like this?"

"Never mind the clever remarks," Jake said. "She needs to see a doctor right away."

The officer eyed her appraisingly. "As long as she's still on her feet and able to walk, it'll have to wait," he finally decided. "I'm taking you both in, along with every other yahoo in the place."

"I'm the one who called you to begin with, you fool!" Jake snapped. "If you want to harass someone, go after the guy behind the bar who makes a habit of serving liquor to minors. Or the lout over there, with the bloody nose, who gets his kicks out of beating up women half his size. We'll be pressing assault charges against him, in case you're interested, but not before the morning."

"You'll do it now, and keep a lid on your temper while you're at it," the other man cautioned. "I'm ticked off enough as it is."

"It's all right, Jake," Sally said, sensing the anger simmering in him. "I don't mind going down to the station and making a statement. I've done nothing wrong."

The patrolman rolled his eyes wearily. "That's what they all say."

"Maybe *they* all do, but in my case, Officer," she told him, staring him down with as much dignity as she could drum up, considering one eye was swollen half-shut, "it happens to be the truth."

Jake touched his finger lightly to her cheek. "All it'll take is a phone call to my lawyer to have things postponed until morning, Sally. You've been through enough for one night."

And she'd have done it all again if, at the end of it all, he looked at her as if she held his heart in his hands, and cushioned her next to him, prepared to defend her to the

death, if need be. It made her wonder if she was hurt more
than she realized, had even suffered minor brain damage,
that she was so ready to forget the terrible price she'd paid
for loving Jake in the past.

Steeling herself not to weaken, she said, "I'd rather get
it over with, if you don't mind."

He shrugged. "Wait here, then, while I collect your coat,
and we'll be on our way." He tipped a glance at the police
officer. "Is it okay if I drive us in my own vehicle, or are
you going to insist we get carted off in the paddy wagon?"

"How much have you had to drink?"

"Half a beer."

"Okay. Take your own vehicle. But just in case you're
thinking of pulling a fast one, I'll be following right on
your tail."

It was past ten by the time they'd signed their statements
at the police station and Sally had been checked over in
the Emergency Room of Eastridge Bay Hospital, and closer
to half past before Jake finally drew up in front of the guest
cottage. By then, the pain in her face and the throbbing
headache which accompanied it had subsided to a dull roar,
thanks to the medication prescribed by the doctor on duty.

"Come on," Jake said, shutting off the engine and flinging open his door. "Let's get you inside and into bed."

"Jake" and "bed" were not a combination she could
handle with equanimity at that point. "I can manage on my
own," she informed him, feeling as if her mouth were
stuffed with absorbent cotton balls.

He laughed, not very kindly she thought. "You're doped
up to the eyebrows, honey. I doubt you can even stand
unassisted."

"Oh, really?" Determined to prove him wrong, she managed to open her door and swing both feet out. Not very
gracefully, to be sure, but they landed in the snow more or

less where she intended they should. "Watch me!" she said, and tried to lever the rest of her body out, only to discover her legs possessed the vertical stability of tapioca pudding.

"Lucky for you that I am," he said, hauling her upright before she made a complete fool of herself. "Where's your house key?"

"Behind the passenger seat of your car...in the front pocket of my briefcase."

"That figures." He strode up the steps to the covered front veranda and propped her against the railing. "Think you can hold on long enough for me to go back and get it?"

"Do I have any choice?" she muttered, far from certain, but fortunately he made short work of the job and soon returned with her briefcase and keys.

He propelled her into the cottage, booted the door closed and waited while she flicked on the switch to his left. The twin sconces on either wall filled the front hall with mellow light and flung soft, welcoming shadows across the floor of the living room.

She'd never been so happy to come home, never so ready to climb onto the big feather bed in the room at the back of the house, and sink into sleep. "You can go now," she told him.

"Sure thing, Sally. Just as soon as you're tucked in for the night."

Marching her into the living room, he dumped her on the sofa in front of the fireplace. "Stay put. I'll be back."

As though from a great distance, she heard him moving about the house. Heard the furnace growl to life in the basement, and water running in the kitchen. Saw through the window the glimmer of stars between the bare branches of the ancient elms bordering her parents' property. Smaller

stars than those in St. Lucia, and not hanging nearly as
close to earth. But spinning...spinning...in lazy, hypnotic
circles....

Her bedroom was large and elegant, like everything else to
do with the Winslow estate, including quarters intended for
short-term occupancy only. Satin smooth oak floors, rich
Oriental rugs, some sort of silk paper the color of old parch-
ment on the walls, and woodwork painted glossy white
weren't too tough to take. Jake had spent the night in far
less luxurious surroundings, and with a lot less desirable
company.

Not that Sally knew he was there, or that he'd stripped
her down to her underwear before putting her to bed. The
pills she'd swallowed at the hospital had finally kicked in
and she was about as dead to the world as was safe, given
her condition.

"She can't be left alone tonight," the E.R. doctor had
warned him. "Someone has to wake her every couple of
hours and if she doesn't respond, get her back here on the
double. The X rays didn't show any fractures, but I'm not
ruling out a possible concussion. She's very lucky she got
off as lightly as she did."

So was the savage who'd used her as a punching bag.
Damned lucky!

A comfortable armchair with a footstool, both on casters,
stood beside the window. Rolling them over the rug to a
spot next to the bed, Jake eased himself into the chair and,
with a grimace, lifted his leg onto the stool. Packing a semi-
conscious woman up a flight of steps to the front door, and
from one room to another—even a featherweight like
Sally—wasn't part of his rehab program, and he was paying
dearly for it.

On the other hand, he ought to be grateful. If he hadn't
been hampered by injury, he'd probably be behind bars
now. The blind urge to kill the brute who'd gone after her

had been tempered not by prudence but by his own physical limitations.

Even now, thinking back to the moment he'd returned to the roadhouse and realized who it was being smacked around the dance floor, filled him with such a flaming rage that he could taste it. It would be a long time before he was able to erase the image of that hamlike fist raised above her head, before he could forget his first sight of Sally's battered face. And a whole lot longer before he forgave himself for being the one most responsible for what had happened to her.

This wasn't how the evening was supposed to end, with him no nearer finding the answers he sought, but altogether too close for comfort to finding himself caught up again in a web of feelings for Sally Winslow. He didn't want to care about her. As a couple, they'd been over for a very long time.

But watching her breathe, seeing the gentle rise and fall of her small, perfect breasts, and recalling how she'd felt beneath his hands when he'd undressed her, a few minutes earlier, filled him with restless yearning. And too many memories.

She'd always had skin like cream. Always been so slender, he could span her waist with his hands. Always smelled like a meadow full of wild flowers under a summer sky, even tonight, after she'd put in a full day teaching, and been rolled around that stinking roadhouse floor.

But that's all they were: memories of a yesterday that could never be recaptured. Because they weren't the same people anymore. Too many years and too many mistakes had come between them. So how crazy was he to want to lie beside her now, and hold her safe in his arms until a new and better tomorrow dawned?

She stirred and moaned softly, bringing him upright in the chair. He lowered his bad leg to the floor with gingerly care and bent over her. Smoothed the dark, silky hair away from her brow, and winced again at the purple bruise discoloring her face. "Sally?"

She opened her eyes and smiled at him, a soft, unfocused smile that stabbed him as sharply as a knife. It was how she used to smile at him after they'd made love. "Hi," she murmured fuzzily.

What's- your life been about all these years we were apart, Sally? he wondered. *How many men have there been since me? How many broken hearts littered along the way?*

She drifted back to sleep with the smile still on her lips. Would that he could've shut off his thoughts so easily! But the door had been opened a crack, and it was enough for all the questions he'd suppressed for so long to come rushing through.

What happened to change things between us, Sally? he asked her silently. *Was the French guy who replaced me a better lover? Did he promise you more than I did? Is that why you put such a definitive end to us? Or we were both too young to realize how fragile love is, and just didn't know enough to take care of it properly?*

CHAPTER FOUR

RELUCTANTLY, Sally struggled through befuddled layers of sleep, loath to forfeit the dreams still chasing her, of a voice—*his* voice, deep and gravelly—murmuring endearments as his hands moved over her limbs and along her shoulders, soothing...healing...captivating. But the flat, white light from outside, a sure sign that yet more snow was falling, splashed insistently against her closed eyelids, telling her it was morning and long past the time to be indulging in dreams.

How could that be? On school days, she awoke at six-thirty, hours before sunrise. Even stranger, how come the aroma of freshly brewed coffee floated on the air?

Puzzled by the amount of effort it took, she turned her head and squinted at the digital clock on the nightstand. *Nine forty-five?* Couldn't be! Classes started at eight-thirty. Academy policy dictated that faculty arrive on campus no later than eight, and good old Tom Bailey put a black mark next to the names of those who didn't observe the rules. Quite what punishment he'd mete out to a teacher who missed the first two classes of the day was enough to boggle even the clearest mind.

Wondering why so slight a movement tugged painfully at one side of her face, why she felt as if she'd been run over by a truck, why the alarm hadn't wakened her at the usual hour, she ventured another glance at the clock just as the display rolled over to nine forty-six. Despite her oddly blurred vision, there was no mistaking the number.

Appalled, she threw back the covers and swung her legs to the floor, intending to make a dash for the bathroom and

51

let a very brief but very hot shower chase away the peculiar fog still swirling in her head. But all that washed over her was a river of pain so ferocious that she sank back on the mattress with a stifled moan.

She hurt everywhere. *Everywhere,* from her head to her feet. Even her teeth ached. And as she fought to contain the myriad pinpoints of agony assaulting her, memories of the previous evening rushed in with equal brutality and left her gasping all over again.

Tentatively she touched her face. Her left cheek was as puffed up as the little lemon cakes which Edith, her mother's housekeeper, sometimes baked for afternoon tea, and felt shiny-smooth as if the skin were stretched too tightly.

Trying not to jar her tender flesh any more than was absolutely necessary, she staggered to the dresser at the foot of the bed, looked in the mirror and almost fainted. The face peering back was barely recognizable: swollen, discolored, and with one eye so bloodshot that she cringed at the sight.

Just then, the faint squeak of wheels approaching down the hall drew her attention. A second later, Jake appeared, pushing the brass tea wagon normally kept in the dining room. He was barefoot, his blue shirt hung open over his navy slacks, his hair was damp and his jaw newly shaved. In short, he looked as casually polished and perfect as she looked damaged and unkempt!

"Uh-uh, none of that," he admonished, parking the trolley to one side and turning her away from the mirror. "Get back into bed, right now, and that's an order."

If it hadn't been for the fact that he was less interested in looking at her ravaged face than at the rest of her, she'd have told him she didn't take orders from anyone, not even a man of his elevated military status. But the attentive way his gaze swept her from head to toe brought home the fact that she was standing there practically naked, and had no memory at all of having undressed herself, the night before. That her bra and panties barely covered the parts he found most engrossing was all the incentive required to send her scurrying back to bed as nimbly as possible.

"How did I get like this?" she asked suspiciously, pulling the covers up to her chin.

He regarded her gravely. "Are you saying you don't remember being at the roadhouse, or the guy who—?"

"Not that," she interrupted. "Of course I remember *that!* I'd have to be brain dead not to! I'm talking about how I came to be here with hardly any clothes on."

"I took the rest off."

Oh, good grief! "When?"

"While you were passed out."

The mere idea almost gave her an aneurism. "Isn't that a bit kinky, especially for a recently bereaved husband?"

He rolled the tea wagon up beside the bed and tried to hand her a glass of orange juice. "No need to fret, sweet Sally. I didn't peek at any naughty bits, if that's what's got you all in a lather. But what if I had? It's not as if I haven't already seen the way you're put together, more times than I can count—although I must admit you've filled out a bit since the last time, and in all the right places and to exactly the right degree, I might add."

"I really don't care what you think," she said, stifling the tingle of delight inspired by his words. "And I don't want any juice, so please stop shoving it at me. What I *do* want is an explanation of just what you're still doing here in my house."

"Juice first, conversation later. And swallow this while you're at it." He pushed the glass at her again, along with a little white pill.

She inspected it skeptically. "What's this?"

"Not an aphrodisiac, if that's what you're hoping. It's

bona fide pain medication prescribed by the doctor who treated you last night.'' Then, sensing she was still inclined to balk, he added, ''Don't give me grief on this, Sally. I'm not in the mood for it. You're not the only one who had a lousy night. That chair might be comfortable enough for an hour or two of reading, but it's not designed for sleeping.''

''I didn't ask you to stay here and baby-sit.''

''Now that,'' he said, sounding decidedly testy, ''is what I call ingratitude! A second ago, you made light of not being brain dead, but it's nothing to joke about. You came very close to being badly injured last night.''

''And whose fault is that?''

''Mine,'' he said. ''And I feel like a big enough jerk, without you rubbing it in.''

She looked away, ashamed. Not everything that had happened last night was crystal clear in her mind, but the fury and horror she'd seen on his face when he came to her rescue was etched indelibly on her memory. ''Sorry. That was uncalled-for.''

He shrugged. ''Down the pill and the juice, Sally. Breakfast is getting cold.''

She saw then that, in addition to juice and coffee, he'd brought in poached eggs and toast, and that he'd made enough for two. ''I appreciate all the trouble you've taken, Jake, but I really don't have time for this. I've already missed my morning classes. Tom Bailey will be fit to be tied.''

''And you'll be missing this afternoon's, too. In fact, he's going to have to manage without you for a few days, as I made clear when I phoned the school first thing this morning—and those are doctor's orders, not mine.'' He touched her bruised cheek with a gentle fingertip. ''In any case, you've seen how you look. What sort of a stir do you think you'll create, showing up with a black eye and half your face swollen to the size of a balloon?''

Of course, he was right. Even if her students didn't mind her appearance, she was pretty sure Tom would. A member of his staff showing up looking as if she'd gone ten rounds with a heavyweight boxing champion was hardly something he'd condone and, in all truth, she didn't feel up to challenging him on it.

Still mindful of her state of undress, she poked one arm out from beneath the covers. "Will you at least hand me my robe? It's hanging on the back of the bathroom door."

He did as she asked, helped her slip her arms in the sleeves so that she looked reasonably decent and fluffed the pillows at her back. A stranger looking in the window might have mistaken him for a devoted husband caring for his ailing wife.

"That's more like it." He nodded approval as she washed down the pill with a mouthful of juice, and tackled her poached eggs. "You'll feel a whole lot better with something in your stomach. You're kind of skinny overall, you know. Do you eat properly, or are you one of those women who live on tofu and celery?"

"I eat like a horse," she informed him, enjoying the food more than she was prepared to admit, even though chewing caused her some discomfort. "And I thought you said I'd filled out in all the right places."

The way he smiled at her spelled trouble she couldn't afford. "It's not where you've filled out that I'm talking about, Sally. It's the rest of you."

"That's what comes of living on a tropical island for years," she said lightly.

"You were short of food?"

"No, but I led a pretty active life. Lots of swimming, scuba diving, beach volleyball and tennis, in my time off."

He poured their coffee, then eased himself onto the side of the bed and started in on his own eggs. "You had plenty of friends, then?"

"A fair number. The ex-pat community was quite large."

"Men friends?"

"Some."

"Any serious involvements?"

"That stopped being any of your business a very long time ago."

"Yes," he said. "There was never much doubt about that, was there?"

Curiosity had her wanting to ask him what prompted him to look so grim as he spoke, but prudence told her to leave the matter alone. Revisiting their shared past was a point-less and dangerous pursuit, threatening not just to open old wounds but also to expose secrets she could never share with him. Better to stick to more neutral territory. "I wasn't lucky enough to find anyone who made me want to exchange the single life for married bliss."

He shrugged. "Marriage has its drawbacks. Not every-one's cut out for it."

But you were, Jake! You just didn't want to share it with me. And even now, it hurts to think how easily you passed me over for someone else.

She pushed aside her plate, her appetite fading a lot faster than her memories. "Thank you for making breakfast. I'm sorry I can't do it justice."

"You're welcome. More coffee, before I clear every-thing away?"

She shook her head and blinked, horrified to find his kindness sweeping her to the brink of tears. The medication must be playing havoc with her emotions; she hadn't wept for him in years.

Watching her altogether too closely, he said, "Is there anything else you'd like?"

To rewrite history, perhaps, but it would take a miracle to achieve that.

"A bath." She ran her fingers through her hair. Felt the grit against her scalp, and shivered with revulsion. "I want to scrub away the grime from last night."

"Understandably." He leaned toward her and went to pull back the bedcovers. "I'll give you a hand."

"You will not!" she said, clutching them against her breast. "I can manage perfectly well on my own."

She thought he was going to argue the point, but after a moment's indecision, he contented himself with, "Fine—as long as you leave the bathroom door open."

"Forget it! You're not—"

"It's not negotiable, Sally. Either the door stays open, or you stay in bed. And in case you're harboring any ideas about thwarting me on this, you should know I helped myself to a shower this morning, while you were still sleeping, and happened to notice the lock on the door can be opened from the outside."

She glared at him, frustrated. "Isn't there some other place you should be? Some tiny detail elsewhere that desperately requires your immediate attention?"

"Nothing that can't wait," he said implacably. "So, are we agreed we'll do things my way?"

She capitulated from sheer exhaustion. "Whatever! Anything for a peaceful life."

"Good girl." He limped over to the dresser. "Tell me where to look and I'll get you a clean nightgown."

"No, thanks! I don't want you fiddling around in my drawers."

He didn't offer a verbal reply. But the glance he cast over his shoulder—long and enigmatic—conferred a provocative subtext to her words which made her blush. She could only pray her multicolored bruises disguised the fact.

To give him credit, he didn't intensify her embarrassment further. "Suit yourself," he said mockingly, wheeling the tea wagon to the door. "While you're cleaning up, I'll don my little apron and do the same to the dishes. Call if you need help.''

The minute he disappeared, she crawled out of bed, collected fresh underwear and a soft cotton nightshirt and fled to the bathroom. She turned on the faucet and tossed a generous handful of aromatic bath salts into the jetted tub— a long, deep luxurious affair designed for leisurely soaking—and, while it filled, stepped under the shower to shampoo her hair and scrub away the worst of the grime.

Then, feeling halfway presentable again, she set the timer on the spa controls, climbed into the tub and immersed herself up to the chin in water so hot she'd probably look like a boiled lobster when she got out. But she didn't care. With her inflatable daisy pillow supporting her neck, and the soothing pulse of the power jets massaging her aching muscles, she'd have been happy to spend the next several hours in such splendid isolation.

Too soon, though, Jake's voice intruded from the other side of the door, an unpleasant reminder that she wasn't entirely in charge of her own destiny at that moment. ''You've been in there long enough, Sally,'' he said, raising his voice to be heard over the noise of the spa motor. ''Time to hop into bed again.''

''Go away,'' she told him irritably. ''I'll come out when I'm ready, and not before.''

He rattled the doorknob, a signature warning that her defiance would exact a price she might not care to pay. ''Don't push your luck!''

As if in cahoots with him, the timer control gave a little *ping,* and the jets dwindled into the same expectant silence emanating from the other side of the door. Recognizing that, in this instance at least, he had the upper hand, she let out a long-suffering sigh. ''Oh, all right! You win this round.''

Surprisingly, instead of crowing over his victory, he accepted it without further comment. She heard his uneven tread as he crossed the bedroom, followed by the sound of the door closing and his footsteps fading as he made his way back to the kitchen wing.

She didn't wait to find out how long he'd be gone, or what he planned to do when he returned. Seizing the moment, she hauled herself out of the tub, toweled herself dry and dressed as quickly as possible.

Just as well she didn't waste any time. She'd barely finished doing up the buttons on her nightgown before the bedroom door was flung open again. "I'm just about ready," she called, flicking a comb through her hair. "If you'd given me another minute instead of being so impatient, I'd have been back in bed again and you'd have nothing to complain about."

The silence which greeted that remark was, she thought, rather ominous. And as soon as she came out of the bathroom, she discovered why. Jake was not the only one waiting for her to put in an appearance. Her mother and sister were there, too, and it was obvious from the latter's scandalized expression that she'd leaped to all the wrong conclusions about exactly what was going on.

Her all-encompassing gaze darted from Sally's attire, to the rumpled bedcovers, to Jake's sweater lying on the floor next to the armchair and, finally, on a heaving breath of indignation, to Jake himself. "Did you spend the night here?"

"Not in the sense that you're implying," he replied coolly.

"And what sense is that, may I ask?"

"As if you'd barely missed finding your sister and me rolling around between the sheets and going at it like a pair of demented rabbits."

Margaret was unaccustomed to being confronted so bluntly and, at the look on her face, Sally couldn't repress a little chirp of laughter. If she'd thrown a lighted match into a can of gasoline, the result couldn't have been more explosive.

Margaret rounded on her in fine fury. "You'll be laughing on the other side of your face when word of your latest escapade reaches certain quarters! I managed to keep it from Tom at breakfast, but he's sure to have heard about it by now, and if you think it's not going to cost you your—"

Distressed, their mother said, "Will you, for heaven's sake, stop fussing about things that aren't important and pay attention to what matters, Margaret? Frankly I'm grateful to Jake. Any fool can see Sally needed someone to look after her through the night, and since none of us knew she'd been hurt, I'm glad he was here to take on the job." She touched her hand lovingly to Sally's bruises. "I'm so sorry, darling. I didn't know what had happened until I saw this morning's paper."

"I made the news?"

"Oh, you did more than that," Margaret huffed, waving the *Eastridge Daily News* under her nose. "It wasn't enough that you made the front page last week, with the daughter of one of this town's leading families winding up dead because of it. No, you had to do it again this week— and involve her husband, if you please!—just to remind everyone how much you enjoy creating a sensation. Once again, you've humiliated all of us with your outrageous behavior and I, for one, have had enough of it. Don't expect me to rush to your defense again, Sally Winslow. This time, you're on your own."

"Which is exactly what I'd like to be right now…left on my own."

"Well, never let it be said I don't know how to take a hint!" Margaret made a grand exit, slamming the front door behind her as a final exclamation point to her annoyance.

Their mother, though, didn't budge. "Either you convalesce up at the main house, Sally, or I'm sending Edith down here to play nursemaid. But you will *not* be left alone until I'm satisfied you're on the mend and able to look after yourself again."

"Glad you're taking that attitude, Mrs. Winslow," Jake said, scooping up his sweater. "Someone needs to crack a whip around this daughter of yours. The hospital staff were adamant that she be watched for twenty-four hours, but she's a difficult patient, as I expect you already know."

"Oh, yes!" She rolled her eyes. "The tales I could tell, if we only had the time. But I can see you're anxious to be off."

Anxious? Desperate was more like it, judging from the way he was edging toward the door. "I do have a few things to take care of," he said.

"I'm sure. What a terrible homecoming you've had, Jake. But thank you for everything you've done. We're very grateful, aren't we, Sally?"

"Yes," she said meekly, willing to agree to just about anything, if it put an end to being badgered. In truth, her head was pounding again and the prospect of crawling back into bed growing more attractive by the minute.

"Then I'll leave you to it." He bathed her in a smile so reminiscent of the old days that she went weak at the knees. "Try to behave yourself, okay?"

"Such a nice man," her mother observed, straightening the sheets and ushering her back to bed as the front door thudded closed behind him. "When you're feeling better, you'll have to tell me what possessed you to go out with him last night, and to that disreputable roadhouse, of all places, because you know, darling daughter, Margaret *does* have a point. It really doesn't enhance your reputation to be seen frequenting such an establishment."

"Yes, Mom. I'm sure you're right. It won't happen again."

Not up to another lecture so soon after the first, Sally closed her eyes, and found it surprisingly easy to slide back into that other, dreamlike world of drifting clouds and deep, restful silence.

A few times in the hours which followed, she sensed that Edith hovered nearby. Once, she was aware of the house-keeper's arm supporting her, of sipping a cool drink and swallowing another pill. But mostly she slept, while her body healed itself.

Sally wasn't the only one targeted for criticism. Colette Burton showed up at Jake's door shortly after he got home, and voiced her displeasure loud enough for half the neigh-borhood to hear.

"How could you be so disrespectful?" she howled, shak-ing the morning paper in his face as she stormed past and took up a position in the middle of the opulent foyer. "My daughter adored you, Jake. You were her whole life. It would break her heart if she knew how soon you'd taken up with someone else a *mere week after her death!*" She dissolved into noisy sobs. "And with *that woman,* of all people! Do you have any idea of the damage you've done to your reputation?"

Given what he suspected and the little bit he'd learned the night before, he'd have liked to tell her that the repu-tation most in danger of being irreparably tarnished was Penelope's. He took no pleasure in inflicting pain, though, so he contented himself with saying mildly, "Things aren't always as they seem, Colette. My reasons for being with Sally Winslow last night were strictly business."

"At some low-class tavern?" She sniffed scornfully, and he could hardly blame her. It *was* a pretty lame reason. "What kind of fool do you take me for?"

He shrugged. "If you choose not to believe me, there's not much I can do about it."

"You can try behaving in a manner befitting a man recently widowed. It might lend more credibility to your protests. Your whole attitude since you came back from overseas is creating comment, Jake. You've been cold and distant to the point of outright cruel. You didn't shed a single tear at the funeral. You ignored my express wishes and flaunted Sally Winslow in our faces afterward." She shook the newspaper again and stared at him, hollow-eyed. "And now, only three days later, we're presented with this! What are we supposed to think?"

"That there might be more to the situation than you realize."

Her tears stopped abruptly, replaced by a shifty wariness. "What do you mean? What are you trying to do?"

"Find some peace of mind."

"At my daughter's expense? I'll see you hung out to dry, first!"

"Don't put words in my mouth, Colette. And don't threaten me."

Her expression slid from cunning to soulful. "Threaten you? Jake, I'm trying to help you!"

"Concentrate on helping yourself," he said. "We each deal with tragedy differently. Accept that your way isn't necessarily the same as mine."

"We should be supporting each other through this terrible time, not struggling through our grief in isolation. There must be something I can do."

"There is," he said. "You can explain why you saw fit to come here and remove Penelope's personal items, instead of leaving me to take care of them. And you can tell me why the coroner's office was directed to send the autopsy results to Fletcher's office, instead to me."

"Why, to spare you, of course! You've been through so

much in the last six months, Jake, and coming home at last, only to be faced with so many sad reminders, didn't seem fair. We wanted to take as much off your shoulders as possible. It's not as if there's any secret about how Penelope died, so why expose yourself to the unpleasantness of the coroner's report? And as for her things, well, sorting through a woman's clothing and deciding what to do with them isn't something most men would want to tackle. If it's her jewelry you're worried about—?''

"I'm not,'' he said. "I have no use for it or her clothes. What I'm trying to say, as tactfully as I know how, is that you're interfering in matters which are not your concern.''

"Penelope was our daughter!''

"Yes. But as you keep reminding me, she was also my wife.''

Nostrils flaring with indignation, she pulled on her gloves and wrenched open the front door. "I'm sorry you see it that way, Jake. I had thought we were family and, as such, deserving of the privileges that entails. Obviously I was wrong. I'll stay out of your way, in the future.''

He knew what he was supposed to do next: refuse to let her leave; beg her forgiveness; tell her she'd always be an important part of his life and prove it by giving her free run of the house. It was the kind of price she exacted from poor old Fletcher, any time he dared disagree with her or exert a little independence. But she'd picked the wrong man, this time.

"Regrettable, but perhaps unavoidable,'' he said, standing aside so as not to impede her exit. "Goodbye, Colette. I'll be in touch if there's anything else we need to discuss. Give Fletcher my best.''

She didn't quite snort in his face. She'd have thought that beneath her. Instead she spat, "You'll be sorry you've taken this tack with me, Jake—you and Sally Winslow, both! You've been away more than you've been home over the last few years, so you may have forgotten how much influence I wield in the upper echelons of this town's social hierarchy. You'll find flouting convention a lot more costly than you seem to realize. Doors which, in the past, have been wide-open to you will be slammed shut in your face. You'll become as much a social outcast as your tacky little tart.''

Not about to get involved in further mud-slinging, he inclined his head dismissively and closed the door on her. No point in retaliating by acquainting her with the knowledge that, from everything he'd so far uncovered, the only tart in the picture appeared to be the one he'd married. Even he drew the line at burdening his in-laws with that kind of information.

But his speaking so bluntly had undoubtedly landed Sally in more trouble than that in which she already found herself. He harbored no illusions about the roasting they'd both receive, the next time his mother-in-law got together with her martini-swigging lady friends.

In all fairness, he had to warn Sally. But not yet. Not until she was on the mend. And definitely not until he'd wormed out of her the information she was so bent on keeping from him.

Oh brother! Landing a fighter jet on the deck of an aircraft carrier was a piece of cake compared to navigating the minefield he'd found waiting for him at home. It was enough to make a guy wish he'd signed up for another tour of duty.

Honorable military discharge might have a fine illustrious ring to it, but it was no guarantee of peaceful retirement. He was still up to his ears in war!

CHAPTER FIVE

HE WAITED four days then, after dark so as not to give rise to any more scandal, went back to the Winslow guest house. A single-story structure designed along the same turn-of-the-century lines as the main mansion, it sat about forty feet inside the driveway, clearly visible to passing traffic or anyone on foot. Not that there was ever much of either in that secluded section of The Crescent, but he deemed it wiser not to draw attention to his presence by driving through the double gates and parking outside her front door.

Instead he left his car on the road, and passing through a smaller side gate set in the wall enclosing the five acre property, approached the cottage. A faint light from the living room to the left spilled out over the garden. His arrival muffled by the snow underfoot, Jake veered off the path leading to the covered porch and looked through the undrawn drapes at the sight within.

Although the rest of the room hovered in shadows, the flickering flames in the hearth and a small table lamp in the corner showed Sally crouched in a chair in front of the fire, with her knees drawn up under her chin. She wore what appeared to be a dark green robe and fluffy white slippers, and even though her hair had swung forward to obscure her face, he sensed her despondency.

As it had at the Burtons' the day of the funeral, and again at the roadhouse the other night, an almost feral urge to rush in and chase away her demons swept over him. Suppressing it, he mounted the steps and pulled the old-fashioned bell chain hanging on the wall beside the door.

When she answered, he waved a large paper sack under her nose. "Before you tell me to take a hike, get a whiff of this. Takeout from the Japanese restaurant on Beach Street, guaranteed to chase away the winter blues."

She sniffed obediently and cast him a glance from beneath her lashes. "Did you bring saké, too?"

"Naturally."

Without another word, she took the bag, gestured him across the threshold, and made tracks for the kitchen.

He tossed his jacket over a brass hook on the coat stand, shucked off his boots, and followed her. "I didn't expect you to capitulate quite that easily, Sally."

"I can't afford to be choosy about the company I keep. Friends are in short supply right now."

"Should I take that to mean you've had another run-in with your sister?"

"Sister and brother-in-law both!" she said, opening the various cartons of food. "Oh, goody! Sticky rice, sauces and chicken yakatori—and shrimp tempura, too! Yum yum!"

Not bothering to hide his grin, he said, "I take it you haven't eaten dinner yet?"

She wrinkled her nose. "It's not that I didn't have the chance, but if I never see beef broth again, it'll be yet too soon. I emptied the last batch down the sink."

"Ungrateful wench!" he chided, breaking the seal on the bottle of rice wine. "Don't suppose you happen to own a set of those little Japanese serving sets for this stuff?"

"Naturally," she said, mimicking the tone of his reply when she'd asked if he'd brought saké, and reaching into the back of a cupboard, brought out a porcelain flask and two little cups etched with graceful white cranes in flight on a celadon background. "This kitchen is nothing if not well-stocked for every occasion. Will you get the tea wagon? We might as well cart everything through to the living room and eat by the fire.''

She turned toward him as she spoke, and in the brighter light of the kitchen, he saw that although the swelling on her face had subsided, the bruises were still livid. Stunned at the fresh uproar of fury to which they gave rise, he did as she asked, glad of any diversion which provided a chance for him to wrestle his emotions under control again.

''You might like to know that the brute who attacked you is behind bars and likely to stay there,'' he told her, rolling the wagon from the dining room to the kitchen counter, and loading the food and plates while she heated the wine. ''He was refused bail—too many previous assault charges. He'll get the book thrown at him, this time.''

''I'll try to draw comfort from that as I figure out my next move.''

He'd have preferred not to acknowledge how uncomfortably depressing he found her answer, but it refused to go ignored. ''Don't tell me you're thinking of leaving town again.''

She tilted her shoulder in a delicate shrug. ''That wasn't exactly what I meant, but now that you mention it, why not? It would seem that, all my good intentions notwithstanding, I'm a source of annoyance or embarrassment to everyone I keep trying so hard to please. What's to keep me here?''

''There's me,'' he heard himself say, before the folly of such an admission could make itself felt. Sheesh, what was it about being near her that brought out the idiot in him? And how come he wasn't fighting harder to conquer it?

''You've got enough to deal with.''

''I've always got time for an old friend.''

Her mouth drooped again in melancholy and he'd have touched her, if she'd let him. Slung a platonic arm around her shoulder and given her a bracing, brotherly hug, as much to convince himself he was in charge of his emotions as to comfort her. But she edged away from him to pour the hot saké into the flask which was, perhaps, a wise move on her part. Touching her under any pretext was as risky as playing football with a live bomb, and he'd be a fool not to admit it.

"Really?" She gave him a blast from those incredible green eyes which never had known how to hide her innermost feelings. "Is that why I neither saw nor heard from you in the last four days?"

"It wasn't from lack of interest on my part, Sally," he said, aching to cup her jaw and trace the sweet, sad curve of her mouth with his thumb. "I thought it best to wait until the ruckus died down some before I came calling again."

"It isn't going to die down, Jake," she said on a quiet sigh. "People in this town have long memories and they don't forgive easily. I was labeled years ago as an incorrigible teenager who abused the privileges to which she was born, and events of the last two weeks have merely confirmed public opinion that I haven't matured into anything much better."

"So you're going to run away?"

She grimaced at the teasing scorn he injected into the question. "Call it that, if you like."

"I *don't* like, Sally!"

"What would you have me do instead? Offer to stand in front of the courthouse, and let the sanctimonious residents of Eastridge Bay pelt me with rotten tomatoes as punishment for my sins, both real and imagined?"

"No," he said, nurturing the anger usurping the maelstrom of less admissible emotions churning his innards. "Prove everyone wrong, instead. Stop groveling for approval and start demanding respect, for a change."

"That won't be easy."

"I never said it would be. Striking out in a new direction takes guts, and I ought to know."

On her way to hold open the kitchen door, she ran her finger over the polished head of his cane, propped against the Welsh dresser, and nodded at his leg. "That's put paid to your military career, then?"

"Yeah. My days flying F-14 Tomcats are over," he acknowledged, managing to steer the loaded tea wagon past her and down the hall to the living room without incident, "but at this rate, I'll make a damn fine butler."

Her laugh, the first genuine sign of amusement he'd heard since he'd met up with her again, floated out to enfold him in memories. They'd laughed a lot in the old days, sometimes freely in pure enjoyment of the moment, and sometimes in the quiet, intimate way that lovers do when only the stars are there to hear.

"Who are you trying to fool, Jake? Our families' roots are as firmly dug into the refined soil of The Crescent as the foundations of their mansions. They don't *produce* servants, they *hire* them."

"Times change, Sally, and we have to change with them."

"Not quite that much! Your father's serving his sixth term as mayor, and your mother's as famous for her elegant soirees as her charity fund-raising." She eyed him thoughtfully as he threw another log on the fire. "And then there's you, a decorated war hero, fresh from the Persian Gulf. Somehow, after all the excitement *that* must have involved, I can't see you settling for the mundane."

He pulled another chair close enough to hers that they could both help themselves from the tea wagon, and poured the saké. "Not so. If war's excitement, I've had enough of it to last me a lifetime. I'm tired of violence." He shot another glance at her bruised face. "I'm tired of seeing innocent victims being subjected to men's brutality."

Ignoring the reference to her own injuries, she said, "You sound burned-out, Jake, and small wonder. Perhaps you just need to do nothing but recover for a while. It's not as if you can't afford it."

He extended his leg and patted the section of thigh just below his hip. "This won't be a problem much longer, and money never has been. My military pension alone's more than enough to keep me afloat, and never mind the investments I made with what I inherited when I turned twenty-one. But I'm not geared for idleness. Once I've got my affairs in order, I'll be ready to take on new challenges."

She dipped a chunk of shrimp tempura in sauce. "And what shape are these challenges going to take? Politics? Law? Finance?"

"Uh-uh." He shook his head. "I'm looking at something a bit more hands-on and down-to-earth than the kind of undertaking my family usually gets involved in."

Her eyebrows shot up in surprise. "Break with tradition, you mean? Good grief, you'll become as much of an outcast as I am!"

"I don't care." Astonished at how easily his thoughts flowed, how ideas which had been fermenting vaguely at the back of his mind for days suddenly took shape and direction, he went on, "I want to build, instead of destroy. Create lucrative jobs for men who don't have much but are willing to put in an honest day's work to earn a dollar. Be remembered as someone who made a difference to ordinary people, instead of that rich guy up on the hill who didn't give a damn about how the other half lived." He flung her an ironic grin. "Feel free to laugh anytime."

"I don't feel like laughing," she said soberly. "You've touched a chord in me. My conscience bothers me in exactly the same way. I've never known want. Never had to wonder where my next meal's coming from, or if, come nightfall, I'd have a roof over my head. Making a difference to people who've never enjoyed the privileges to which I was born is what made working in the Caribbean so rewarding.''

''And you don't find the same kind of satisfaction teaching at The Academy?''

She made a face. ''I guess you haven't heard. I've been relieved of my duties there. Tom stopped by yesterday and delivered the news in person. The Board of Governors doesn't care for the kind of notoriety I bring to the school.''

''I'm sorry, Sally. I'm afraid I'm mostly to blame for that. If I hadn't dragged you to Harlan's Roadhouse—''

She waved aside his apology. ''I'd have found some other way to offend. I don't fit the sort of image they like to project.''

''Maybe not, but that's no reason to let them chase you out of town. There must be other schools looking for teachers.''

''I don't want any other school, any more than I ever wanted The Academy, because I'm not really cut out for teaching. It's something I drifted into because there was a need on St. Lucia for something I could offer, but I'm not passionate enough about it to want to pursue it here. It doesn't inspire me.''

''Funny you should say that. I never could imagine you as a schoolmarm, though I doubt your students would agree with me. I imagine they found you to be an excellent teacher.''

She shrugged and popped a sauce-smeared fingertip into her mouth, then slowly drew it out again, oblivious to the innate sensuality of her action. But he was overwhelmed with stunning recall of the time at the country fair that they'd shared a huge ball of cotton candy and, afterward, she'd licked away the grains of spun sugar sticking to his chin, then let her tongue trace a leisurely path down the length of his throat. He'd been left painfully aroused, and felt the same stirrings threatening his self-control now.

Dragging his gaze away, he shifted in the chair, tried to look unmoved, and said, "So if teaching doesn't light a fire under you, what does?"

She selected a skewer of chicken and regarded it pensively. "Fighting for the underdog," she said at last. "Defending the right to be different of those who don't fit the conventional mold, or who aren't able to defend themselves."

"Pretty lofty ideals, Sally."

"No more so than yours."

"I guess not, but then, we always were on the same wavelength."

Sudden tense silence exploded as palpably as if an unwelcome third party had crashed through the door and cast a paralyzing spell on everything in the room. Even the flames in the hearth seemed to lose their energy.

"No, we weren't," she said, shattering the brittle atmosphere. "Not always."

"If you're referring to the summer you went to Paris, we never did talk about it, and I've often—"

"I see no point in harking back to the distant past."

The warm, animated woman who'd shared his ambitions a moment before changed before his eyes, morphing into a stranger in less time than it took to blink. Just as well. He hadn't come to her house to dig up old bones; they had more current skeletons to uncover.

"Then how about if we clarify a few points about the *recent* past, specifically the events of the other night?" he suggested coolly.

Her eyes grew as secretive and guarded as a forest glade. "To my mind, the only thing that's unclear is how you can justify leaving me to fend for myself in that swill-pot of a bar."

"I can't," he said, "and you've got to know I've cursed myself a thousand times since for what happened to you."

"More to the point, Jake, what happened to *you?* Where did you disappear to?"

"I found a kid of eighteen, drunk out of his mind in the men's room, and drove him home. I figured I'd be back before you had time to miss me. Only problem was, he passed out in the car and his mother thought I was the one who'd been feeding him liquor. By the time we sorted that out and I helped her get him upstairs to bed, it took me fifteen minutes instead of five. But if I'd known that you—"

"There was no way you could have," she interrupted softly. "You did the right thing, helping that boy, and if I didn't forgive you before, I do now."

"But I haven't forgiven myself, and I don't know that I ever will. I was ready to commit murder when I saw what that brute was doing to you. Might have given in to the urge if the police hadn't shown up when they did. Just as well I called them after I left the boy's house to report them serving underage kids." He returned his half-finished meal to the tea wagon, his appetite killed by the ongoing wretchedness which had haunted him for the last four days. "All my fine talk about despising violence doesn't amount to much when the chips are down, does it? I'm still a savage when it comes to defending the woman I l—"

What? *The woman I love?* Is that what he'd almost said? He must be crazy! He hadn't been in love with any woman for years.

Flabbergasted, he leveled a glance at her, expecting to see amusement mirrored on her face, and instead surprising such a look of raw vulnerability that it was all he could do not to leap up and haul her into his arms.

As though she realized she'd betrayed too much of what she was feeling, the color flooded her face. But it was too late for evasive action. Some things time couldn't change, and that instinctive, deep-down knowledge of each other was one of them.

He hadn't needed to finish his sentence for her to figure it out. If uncertainty existed as a result, it was his, because he had no idea why she should find his near-admission so painful.

"What I should have said," he began, stumbling over the words.

But she, recovering more quickly, cut him off. "Is that the built-in male instinct to protect the weaker sex ruled the moment."

"Something like that," he said, and decided it was high time to change the subject. "I went back to the roadhouse yesterday. It's been temporarily shut down for violation of the liquor law, but I tracked down the owner and showed him a photo of Penelope. It took a bit of fiscal persuasion, but he finally admitted she'd been a regular there for months—long before you came back to town."

Sally stared at her bowl of rice as if she feared it might jump up and bite her. "Did he indeed?"

"Mmm-hmm." He watched her closely, but unlike the moment before, she was no longer giving away anything of what she was thinking, so he decided to pull out all the stops. "He went so far as to call her 'a regular little sex terrier in heat.' Not a term I'm familiar with, I admit, but you have to agree, it does paint a telling picture."

"Yes," she said, her voice as flat and unrevealing as the drab winter landscape outside. "I suppose it does."

"You surprise me, Sally," he said mildly. "I expected you to refute any such allegation—and with a lot more vigor than you're presently exhibiting. Which begs the question: Why? How much more do you know that you're not willing to tell me?"

That brought about the results he'd been looking for!

Agitated, she flung down her rice bowl, hurled herself out of her chair, and circled around the furniture to the window, so that he was left staring at her back.

"Why should I know anything?" she said. "She didn't confide in me."

"The pair of you were inseparable once. You knew her better than anyone."

"That was before."

"Before what?"

She pinched her mouth shut, as though she regretted having spoken so rashly, and chose her next words more carefully. "Before we drifted apart. We weren't in regular contact while I was away. I have no idea which places she normally frequented. We went out together only the one time, to catch up on each other's news, and you already know how the night ended. You're a widower because of my recklessness."

"Am I?" he said, hoisting himself to his feet and going after her. "Do you really hold yourself to blame for my wife's death?"

She shied away from him like a nervous foal. "Who else? I was the one driving the car."

"You were driving *her* car which isn't quite the same thing. Care to tell me why?"

"No," she said stubbornly.

"Then I'll tell you. She was too drunk to drive, so you took over. She didn't like the idea. Probably fought you for the keys. How am I doing so far, Sally?"

She didn't reply, nor did she need to. The pallor creeping over her face and made all the more noticeable because of her bruises, said it all.

"You probably had to pour her into the passenger seat," he continued. "And either you didn't notice she hadn't done up her seat belt, or she refused to buckle it, which is why, when you wrapped the car around that power pole, you emerged virtually unscathed, but she was thrown out of the car and killed.''

He'd finally found the key to breaking her silence and once she started talking, she couldn't stop.

"She didn't want to leave the bar," she said, her voice as lost as that of a child trying to outrun a recurring nightmare. "Oh, it was horrible…embarrassing! She made a terrible scene, crawling around on her hands and knees, and swearing. She was like an animal. I hardly recognized her. Didn't want anyone to know I knew her. When I finally got her outside, she dropped her purse and that's how I managed to get the car keys. I had to fight to get her into the car. She was furious…out of control. Lunging to grab the keys out of the ignition. Trying to grab the steering wheel. The car started skidding…I thought the tires would never stop screaming…and I couldn't…I couldn't…!"

"I know you couldn't," he said, hating himself for what he was doing to her, but too driven by his own demons to let the matter rest. "I've been through the same thing with her, more times than I care to count."

"But you didn't end up killing her."

"It was an accident, Sally—one she caused. If you'd let her get behind the wheel of that car, you'd both be dead— and that I couldn't live with."

"I should have stopped her from drinking so much. You must hate me for what I let happen."

Without considering the repercussions to such a move, he closed the remaining distance between them, and reached out to stroke her hair. A blameless enough gesture in itself and intended only to soothe her misery, it backfired disastrously. The strands slipped between his fingers like polished silk, and he found his hand caressing her face instead.

At that, all the restraint, all the tight, unspoken caution between them, disintegrated into ashes, seared by a jolt of awareness so acute that she flinched at its impact. Her hands shot up, as if to shove him away, but she turned toward him instead and clutched at the front of his sweater. She closed her eyes, and let out a stifled moan.

Of defeat? Surrender? It didn't matter. What happened next was beyond her control or his. Their lips came together, guided by tacit yearning, and it was as if yesteryear had never happened. The floodgates opened and let the pent-up longing run free. One second they stood at arm's length from one other, and the next she was crushed against him, and he was punctuating short, frantic kisses with words he had no business thinking, let alone speaking aloud.

"I could never hate you," he muttered, anguished that she'd even entertain the idea. "You were my first love... my best love."

"Don't!" she cried. "You can't say things like that! You just buried your wife."

"I know...I know."

And still he kissed her, stealing his mouth along her jaw and down her throat. And still she let him. Her arms stole around him. Her head fell back, leaving her long, lovely neck exposed to his domination. She trapped his knee between her parted legs, and tilted her hips against him with a desperation which matched his.

She was crying the whole time, and she was beautiful. So beautiful, he could hardly breathe.

"You'll hate us both, tomorrow," she whispered, the tears seeping out from beneath her closed eyelids. "You'll feel such remorse...!"

He raised his lips to trace fleeting kisses over her bruises. "Nothing I've done before or ever might do in the future can equal a tenth of the remorse I feel for what I let happen to you on Monday."

"It wasn't your fault."

"It was my fault." He stroked the ball of his thumb over her tears, tasted the salty tracks they left behind. "And I wanted so badly to make it up to you. Wanted to lie beside you in your bed. Hold you all night long. Keep you safe and never let you go."

"It's because you're in denial over Penelope," she sobbed. "You don't want to accept that she betrayed you. That's why you're saying all this. You just need someone to hold on to, and I happen to be here."

He wished it were so. It would make everything so much easier. But he was tired of pretending to be grief-stricken. Tired of trying to preserve a charade which had played itself out years ago.

"Not just anyone, Sally," he said, rocking her in his arms. "Only you. When we're together, I believe in tomorrow. You make me *feel* again. You make me want to live."

She melted against him, her protests dying on a sigh as he covered her mouth again with his. He stroked his hand down her throat, over the fabric of her robe—some sort of dense silky fabric with a raised, uneven texture. And beneath it, infinitely softer, a thousand times silkier, her skin, smoother than cream.

The scent of her, light, with a trace of vanilla, owed nothing to perfume and everything to the essence of the girl she'd once been and the woman she'd become. He'd have recognized that fragrance anywhere. It beckoned to him just as the aroma of rich, warm food would lure a starving man.

Who knew what might have happened next, if a too-bright light hadn't splashed against the window from outside and revealed them in blatant contravention of everything society held decent?

"What the devil...!"

He swung her behind him, aware that although he could shield her from further physical exposure right then, he could do nothing to prevent the further damage to her reputation later. Whoever had come sneaking up to the house had found what they'd been seeking and he doubted they'd keep it to themselves.

Trying to apprehend the intruder was futile. As swiftly as it had pierced the dim ambience of the room, the flashlight was extinguished. A figure scurried across the snow-covered lawn and down the drive toward the gates. Seconds later, the sound of a car racing down the road split the silence of the night.

"Hell's bells!" Cursing, he yanked the drapes across the window.

"Thank you," she murmured on a frail breath.

"For what? Talk about too little, too late!" He turned back to find her cowering against the chair with her fingers pressed to her lips. "I'm sorry, Sally. I'm afraid whatever problems you thought you had before I showed up here tonight have just multiplied a thousand times over."

CHAPTER SIX

STUNNED, Sally stared at him. "Why do you say that?"

"Think about it," he said, limping to the hall and pulling on his jacket and boots. "What kind of person shines a light through a window to spy on someone, then takes off without explanation? He—or she—wasn't collecting donations for the SPCA, Sally, you can bet on that! They had an ulterior motive in mind."

She trailed after him, still struggling to come to grips with the situation. "Like breaking and entering, you mean?"

He shrugged. "Could be."

"Oh, I don't think so! This is just a guest cottage with nothing much in it worth stealing. Why would anyone bother with it, when there are far richer pickings to be found all over the neighborhood?"

"I rather think the fact that it's *your* cottage is the real issue."

A flutter of alarm quivered up her spine. "That doesn't exactly reassure me, Jake!"

"Sorry. Forget I said anything. I'm as much in the dark as you are." He stepped out onto the front porch. "To be on the safe side, though, lock the door behind me and stay put while I take a look around to make sure whoever it was isn't still hanging around. Might be as well to check all the other doors and windows as well, while you're at it. I'll be back shortly."

She'd never been afraid of living alone before; never seen the guest house as anything but a charming cottage safely set within the grounds of her parents' estate, in an area regularly patrolled by security guards. Petty crime was almost unheard-of in that neighborhood.

Since coming back to town, though, she seemed to be a magnet for trouble. It had dogged her wherever she went, and the strain was beginning to tell. As she made her way from room to room, she found herself jumping at shadows and listening, with her nerves on edge, for any unfamiliar sound.

Suddenly the French doors in the dining room seemed too flimsy to deter an intruder; the low sill of the long window in her bedroom too easily straddled. No fence separated the patio at the back of the house from a thicket of dwarf pines set so closely together that a dozen pairs of eyes could be watching her every move from between the dense branches. And the furnace—had it always made that odd clicking sound, or was someone tampering with the latch at the laundry room window?

A sudden sharp rap at the front door caused her heart to miss a beat, then race with erratic relief when Jake called out, "It's me again, Sally."

She hurried to let him in. "Did you find anything?"

"Just footprints in the snow. The bad news is your uninvited guest tramped over those dwarf shrubs out front. The good news is, he doesn't have very big feet and won't have done too much damage."

"And that's all?" She leaned out and lifted the lid of the mail box hanging on the wall beside the door. "No nasty anonymous note left behind? No brick ready to be thrown through the window?"

"Nothing. Which leads me to deduce this was a spur-of-the-moment sort of thing—most likely some kid showing off for his buddies. It's the kind of thing teenagers do for kicks." He pulled his keys from his pocket and turned up the collar of his jacket. "No big deal, really."

More dismayed than she cared to admit, she said, "And that's it? You're leaving, just like that?"

"Might as well. I'm pretty sure you won't be bothered again tonight, but set the house alarm before you go to bed, just to be on the safe side."

"That's not why I asked." She raised her hands, palms up. "Jake, before we were so rudely disturbed, you and I—"

"Were playing with fire," he said flatly. "You should be grateful we were interrupted. My coming here tonight was a big mistake."

Well, he'd certainly learned how to get his point across plainly! No subtle hints or gradual lessening of interest designed to spare her feelings this time around, just blunt, outright rejection, and to hell with whether or not he left her bleeding!

"I know," she said, injecting her voice with chilly pride. "In fact, if you recall, I tried telling you that, but you wouldn't listen."

"Well, I'm listening now. And I thank you for the reminder."

He deigned to look her squarely in the face then, and just fleetingly she thought she saw pain in his eyes. But if so, it was probably because his leg was hurting. Or his conscience. "Don't forget your cane," she spat, running to the kitchen to retrieve the damned thing and practically throwing it at him. "I'd hate to think you might find a reason to come back again. And who knows, you might need it the next time you have to rush to the defense of a woman you've coerced into accompanying you to the seediest dive in the county."

She was panting for breath by the time she'd finished her tirade. Not that it seemed to impress him any!

"I'm sorry if I've upset you," he said calmly. "You've

had more than enough to deal with lately, without my making things worse.''

''You haven't made things worse, so don't flatter yourself.'' Furious to discover she'd learned *nothing* from past experience, she almost shoved him back onto the porch. ''If anything, I'm grateful to you for reminding me why we didn't last as a couple before. You always had a talent for getting things started, but you never were very good at carrying them through to any sort of decent conclusion.''

''What the devil do you mean by that?''

''Figure it out for yourself,'' she snapped, and without waiting for him to reply, slammed the door shut in his face and turned off the outside light.

So what if he fell down the steps and broke the other leg? It was no less than he deserved! Not that there was much chance that he would. The moon shone so brightly, it cast shadows over the lawn. If he hadn't rendered her half-blind with passion, she'd have seen the prowler approaching long before he'd had the chance to shine his flashlight through the window and catch her on the verge of making the second biggest mistake of her life.

Jake was right on that score: she *was* lucky they'd been interrupted, and in more ways than he could begin to imagine! Being around him made her reckless. She was far too inclined to let things slip—things she'd kept secret for years.

By fair means or foul, he managed to infiltrate her defenses. He brought the past alive again, as vividly as if it had taken place just yesterday. But worse—much worse!— he glossed over the bad parts and persuaded her to remember only the good. In short, he made her forget to be careful.

Seething at the realization, she turned away from the door, intending to go back to the living room to throw out the remains of their meal and anything else which might remind her of him. But as she passed by, she happened to catch sight of herself in the hall mirror.

Appalled, she stared at the vacant-eyed creature confronting her; at her kiss-swollen mouth and the faint red traces of whisker burn along her jaw and down her throat. Her hair lay in wild disarray. The zipper of her robe had slipped down far enough to bare one shoulder and reveal the swell of her cleavage.

In short, she was shown exactly for what she was: weak, contemptible, stupid, and so mired in old misery that she hadn't a hope of outrunning the painful memories chasing her....

Things had started to unravel between her and Jake the September she left for her semester at the Sorbonne in Paris. He'd turned twenty the previous spring, and was halfway through the undergraduate degree required for admission to Naval Aviation Officer Training School. She'd been just eighteen, newly graduated from high school and still glowing from a summer spent with the man she adored with every particle of her being.

Saying goodbye to Jake hadn't been easy, but she'd accepted the opportunity to perfect her French while she pursued her interest in art, in the most romantic city in the world, as fair compensation for being so far away from him.

It wasn't as though they'd have spent much time together if she'd stayed home. The four hundred miles separating them ever since he'd gone off to university, two years earlier, meant they weren't able to see each other very often during the academic year. And although other long-distance relationships might falter, theirs had grown stronger. They had never been more deeply in love. So she'd gone off with an easy mind, sure nothing Europe had to offer could change that.

Nor had it. The changes had come from him—little

things at first, creeping in so subtly that she refused to acknowledge the intuitive dread slowly poisoning her mind.

If he sounded remote and strained over the phone, it was because she was half a world away. If he sometimes wasn't at his apartment when she called him, it was because of his heavy third-year course load and he was probably still at the campus library.

When he suggested cutting back their twice-weekly conversations and relying on email instead, she agreed it would be more convenient, because she didn't want to come across as possessive and insecure. After all, they trusted one another. Implicitly. Didn't they?

If he sometimes took days to acknowledge her messages and then sent only a few noncommittal lines in reply, it had to be because he didn't want anyone else accidentally coming across what he'd written. Either that, or he was preparing for midterm exams and was preoccupied. Understandable enough. Good grades were essential if he was to achieve his career ambitions.

So she continued making excuses and living in a make-believe world, until the day that reality caught up with her.

"The reason your cycle isn't normal has nothing to do with illness, my dear," the kindly French doctor told her when, alarmed by two consecutive months of spotty menstrual bleeding, she finally sought medical advice. "You're about ten weeks pregnant. It happens sometimes with a woman that there's a little show of blood at the time she'd normally have her period. It usually stops after the first trimester and becomes a matter for concern only if the flow increases significantly and is accompanied by cramping."

Her life was spiraling out of control, yet still she tried to delay coming to terms with it. She couldn't tell Jake about the baby. Not yet. It wouldn't have been fair to burden him with news like that by email or telephone. Very soon now, she'd be going home, and they'd be together again.

He'd promised he'd be waiting to meet her flight, that they'd spend the Thanksgiving holiday together, and she'd clung to that. The news could wait until then; until he was holding her in his arms again, and she could see for herself the passion in his eyes which he'd never been able to hide.

But he hadn't been there when she got home, and suddenly there was no longer any denying what her heart had been trying to tell her for weeks. Shattered, she'd confided in Penelope.

"Something's terribly wrong between me and Jake," she'd said, and poured out all her misgivings in the desperate hope that her best friend would laugh and tell her she was imagining things.

Penelope hadn't laughed. She'd looked deeply regretful and said, "Yes, something's wrong. Better brace yourself, Sally."

"Why? What is it?" Fear had clutched at her throat and made it near-impossible for her to breathe. "Is he ill?"

"Hardly! He's seeing someone else. A freshman coed."

It had been as if someone had struck a hammer blow to her heart. For a few seconds, she'd done more than stopped breathing; she'd stopped living. "Where did you hear such a thing?"

"From my cousin Thea. She lives in the same college dorm as his new girlfriend, and she told me when I went to visit her. As a matter of fact, I saw him while I was there, as well. We had lunch together."

"I don't believe it!" Sally had cried, all the while knowing at some deeper level that it was the truth. "I trust him. He'd never cheat on me."

"He's been cheating on you for weeks, Sal. Why else do you think he stopped phoning?"

"Trans-atlantic calls are expensive."

"Don't make me laugh! He could afford to call you three times a day, if he wanted to."

"The time difference makes them inconvenient. We decided we'd write to each other, instead."

"And how long did that last before he grew tired of it?"

She'd clamped a hand to her mouth, afraid she'd become physically ill as the suspicions she'd harbored crystallized into a mass of huge, unmanageable certainty. The tears had rolled down her face in rivers.

Oozing a convincing mixture of sympathy and outrage, Penelope had handed her a box of tissues. "He's such a jerk, Sally. You're well rid of him."

"No, I'm not!" she'd wept. "I love him! And I have to talk to him. There's something he needs to know."

Penelope had sighed. "Talking isn't going to do any good. He won't listen."

"He has to!" Despair getting the better of her, she'd spilled out the awful truth. "Penelope, I'm pregnant!"

"Oops!" Penelope's eyes had opened wide in mock horror. "Is he the father?"

If she hadn't been so devastated, she'd have slapped Penelope for asking such a question. "Of course he's the father!"

"Well, you can't blame me for wondering. You *have* just spent three months in Paris, after all—more than enough time to enjoy a little fling on the side with someone else."

"You know I'd never do that! Jake's the only man I've ever been with."

"Pity he wasn't smart enough to use a condom then, is all I can say."

"He did." She'd laid her hands lightly against her abdomen. "That's why I didn't suspect there'd be a baby in here."

"And you think saddling him with the news now will bring him back? Dream on, girlfriend! These days, men aren't shackled by such old-fashioned notions of honor.

He'll either deny any responsibility for the blessed event, or else cut you a check and tell you to get an abortion."

By then beside herself, she'd wailed, "You're wrong. He'd never leave me to deal with this alone."

"He'll wash his hands of you. Face it, Sally, he's moved on to someone else and you can't count on him for anything anymore." She'd slipped an arm around Sally's shoulders. "But you can count on me. I'll stand by you."

Inconsolable, she'd sobbed, "But I want Jake!"

"Well, he doesn't want you," Penelope told her briskly, "so you'd better learn to live with it."

She'd rather have died than accept such a painful truth, but fate wasn't done with her yet. That night, she started bleeding again, in earnest this time, and by morning she was doubled over with cramps. Heartbroken and ashamed, she'd turned again to Penelope because she couldn't tell her parents. She couldn't have borne their sorrowful disappointment.

Penelope drove her to a hospital in the next town, and waited while she underwent surgery to finish what nature hadn't managed to complete on its own. Penelope comforted her afterward and promised she'd never tell a soul. Penelope took care of everything.

But she couldn't mend a broken heart. Nor could she spare Sally the pain of seeing Jake over the Christmas holidays. She hadn't known he was home, and froze with shock when she bumped into him outside a downtown shop.

He looked wonderful. *Wonderful!* So tall and dark and handsome that she couldn't drag her gaze away. "Oh!" she said, the word puffing out of her mouth on a cloud of chilly condensation. "Oh, hi! What a surprise, running into you like this."

"Yes," he said, and might as well have been a total stranger, he spoke so coldly. "How was Paris?"

"Very French," she replied, somehow managing to smile, even though his attitude left her heart in shreds. "Very exciting. I learned a lot."

"I think we both did—a hell of a lot more than we bargained for."

How could he be so distant? So unmoved? As if she were just a girl he'd known in high school and whose name he barely remembered? "I'm not sure I know what that means," she said, her voice breaking despite herself.

At that, a shadow had crossed his face, and for one insane moment, she thought she'd managed to pierce his formidable reserve and find the boy she used to know.

Elated, she hung on the edge of hope, but too soon crashed down to earth again as the shop door to her left opened, and a petite brunette wearing a scarlet beret and cape came out.

"Sorry to keep you hanging around in the cold, sweetie," she chirped, dangling a beribboned box under Jake's nose, "but I want your gift to be a surprise." Then, noticing Sally, she smiled prettily and said, "Oh, hello! Am I interrupting something?"

"No," Jake said, making a big point of tucking her hand in the crook of his elbow.

Bright-eyed as a baby robin, she glanced from his face to Sally's. "But you know each other, yes?"

"Not anymore," Sally choked, and brushing roughly by them, hurried away.

Concerned by their daughter's despondency over what they believed to be nothing more than a bad case of first love gone wrong, her parents sent her to college in California in January, hoping year-round sunshine and a change of scene would revive her spirits.

She'd been glad to go; glad to get away from all the reminders of the things she'd lost. She'd mourned for a year—for the baby who'd never had a chance to live, and for being gullible enough to believe Jake had ever really cared for her.

Rather than risk running into him again, Sally came home seldom over the next three years, and then stayed only briefly. Penelope, meanwhile, flitted from one exclusive eastern college to another. Weakened by the miles separating them, their friendship dwindled and eventually died.

It didn't matter. New friends eventually replaced the old, and if she didn't entirely forget her previous life, Sally believed the scars had finally healed over. Until she was in the final year of her undergraduate degree, that was, and Margaret sent her a newspaper clipping announcing the marriage of Lieutenant Jake Harrington.

She realized then that she hadn't healed at all. The wound ripped open with a vengeance made all the more painful by the knowledge that his bride was none other than her erstwhile friend, Penelope Jessica Burton....

And now Penelope was dead.

Sally Winslow and Jake Harrington were both in the same town again.

She was as susceptible to him as ever.

And he was still as untrustworthy and heartless.

Impulsively, Sally raised her fist and smashed it against the mirror, wanting to break it and not caring if she cut her hand to ribbons in the process. Wanting only to get rid of the foolish twenty-six-year-old face staring back at her from haunted eyes.

But the mirror only swayed a little on the hook holding it in place. The thick beveled glass didn't crack. And the face reflected in it remained as it was before.

Some things never changed, no matter how much time went by or how much wisdom a person thought she'd acquired.

Disgusted with herself, she turned her gaze aside. What kind of warped individual was she, that she allowed him to

wield such power over her? What did she have to do to cut
the ancient ties which persisted in holding her to him?

As though it had been lying in wait for just such a moment to reassert itself, the familiar answer rang through her
mind, clear as a church bell tolling across the frozen coun-
tryside: *She had only one option. She had to run away
again because, as long as their paths continued to cross,
she'd never be free of him. He would continue to play
havoc with her emotions, her life, her peace of mind.*

The decision made, she ran to the bedroom and flung
open the closet and the dresser drawers, anxious not to
waste another precious moment. She could pack and be on
her way before he had time to realize she was gone.

She'd find another place to put down roots. One far
enough removed from his shadow that it couldn't reach out
to touch her, ever again.

The next morning, she received a subpoena to appear as
chief witness for the prosecution, in the case against Sidney
Albert Flanagan, charged with assault and battery. His trial
date had been set for the beginning of April. Six long weeks
away.

Escape wasn't going to be as quick and painless as she'd
thought, after all.

He knew she was hurt at the way he'd taken off and left
her hanging like that, as if he was glad he'd been given an
excuse to escape. But he'd been so bloody furious at what
he'd discovered when he went outside that he'd hardly been
able to contain himself, and telling her what he'd found
would have upset her more than his running out on her.

If he cared for her at all—and he knew now that his
feelings ran deeper than he'd ever realized, despite everything she'd done in the past—he had to stay away from her
until he'd taken care of a problem which he'd created but

which she was paying for. Because it was pretty clear that he was the reason she'd been targeted the night before.

The tire tracks skimming alongside his car had gouged deep furrows in the snow. Whoever had spied on them had been in one hell of a hurry to leave. Enough that they'd sideswiped his right front fender and left it flecked with scrapings of dark maroon paint.

Nor was that the only clue he'd come across. He'd told Sally the truth when he said he'd discovered footprints on her front lawn. What he didn't disclose was that only a woman with very expensive tastes would wear a winter boot so delicately fashioned and with such a narrow, pointed heel.

He hardly needed supernatural powers to figure that someone had recognized his Jaguar, and stopped to investigate the reason he'd left it parked in the shadow of the wall surrounding the Winslow estate. Or that the someone in question was a rotten driver and owned a dark maroon car. And he'd have had to be brain dead not to be able to put two and two together, and come up with four. Which was why, the next morning, he paid a call on his mother-in-law.

Colette was in the breakfast room when he arrived, shortly after half-past nine, and his most charitable thought when he saw her was that she looked like hell. Wearing a filmy, pale yellow negligee to match her complexion, she drooped over the black coffee poured by the faithful Morton as if she couldn't summon up the strength to lift the delicate china cup.

Jake knew a hangover when he saw one; he'd had plenty of practice with Penelope. Nor had he served six years' active duty in the military without recognizing panic when it was staring him in the face. As soon as she set eyes on him, Colette just about had a stroke!

He slid into the chair opposite hers and helped himself

to coffee. "Sorry to bother you so early, Colette, but I wanted to catch you before you went about your day."

"Why? What do you want?" she inquired faintly, peering at him from bloodshot eyes.

"Well, it's like this," he said, and pasted on his most soulful smile. "I'm planning to send most of the furniture in the house to auction or give it to charity, but if there are any pieces you'd like—"

Colette's eyes welled with tears. "Couldn't you wait a decent interval before you wipe every trace of my daughter from your life?"

"I don't need things to remind me, Colette," he said. "I have other, less tangible souvenirs. And since I plan to move soon—"

"You're selling the house Penelope loved so much?" Outrage left spots of color on Colette's otherwise sallow cheeks. "The house her father and I gave you as a wedding present?"

"It isn't mine to dispose of," he said, with what struck him as admirable restraint. Though a generous gift, the pretentious mansion two blocks away had always been a bone of contention between him and Penelope. He'd never felt at home there and was relieved to be free of it. "It's yours to do with as you see fit. I'm simply moving to something more suited to my needs."

"Whatever they might be!" she shot back nastily.

"Yes," he said. "Whatever they might be—which brings me to the reason I'm here now. My car's been involved in an accident."

"What's that got to do with me?"

"I wondered if you'd thought to check yours," he said, staring idly out at the snow-covered terrace. "I imagine it's a bit banged up, too."

"I haven't the foggiest idea what you're talking about,"

she said loftily. "The only place I went last night was to play bridge at the club."

He swung his gaze back to her and waited a moment to let her absorb what she'd let slip, then said, "Did I specifically mention last night, Colette?"

Her hand started to shake so badly, she had to replace her cup on its saucer. "What I meant is that last night was the *only* time I went out yesterday."

He forbore to add that he hadn't specifically mentioned "yesterday," either, and merely repeated, "To play bridge at the country club."

"I already told you that I did."

"From here," he said conversationally, "the only way to get to the club is to drive along The Crescent."

"Well, yes, Jake," she snapped, and directed an emphatic glance at the carriage clock on the mantel. "Is there a point to all this? I'm in rather a hurry."

To do what, he wondered uncharitably. Fall back into bed and try to sleep off the effects of last night? "Then I'll cut to the chase. I believe you when you say you spent the evening playing bridge at the club."

"Thank you, I'm sure!"

He fixed her in the sort of stare guaranteed to reduce a junior officer to babbling incoherence. "I also believe that, on the way home, you came across my car parked outside the gate to the Winslow property and decided it was your business to find out why. You saw lights in the guest cottage, came sneaking up to see what kind of mischief might be going on, discovered me with Sally, and elected to teach us both a lesson. So you went back to your car, shone a flashlight through the window to leave us in no doubt that we'd been caught misbehaving, and hoped it would be enough to scare her into shutting me out of her life for good."

"That's the most preposterously far-fetched idea I've

ever heard. If you're worried about what to do with your time now that you're no longer with the military, Jake, you should think about writing children's fairy tales.''

''If I've jumped to the wrong conclusions, there's an easy enough way to prove it.''

''And how's that?''

''Show me your car.''

''I will not!'' She tried, but her attempt to project righteous indignation fell badly short of the mark.

''You do realize there's nothing to stop me going to your garage and taking a look for myself?''

''I'll have you thrown off the property first!''

He sighed, his patience at an end. ''I'm not enjoying this any more than you are, so allow me to speak plainly. I waited until I knew you'd be alone before I confronted you because I didn't think you'd want Fletcher knowing what you've been up to. But either we settle this now, or I go straight from here to his office—with a side-trip to the police first, to report a hit-and-run incident incurring several hundred dollars of damage to my very expensive automobile. I don't imagine they'll have any trouble tracking down the perpetrator. Yours, I believe, is the only maroon Lincoln Town Car in the area. It's your call, Colette.''

Her face crumpled and suddenly she looked seventy instead of only fifty-six. ''It's your own fault!'' she said bitterly. ''You and that bitch who killed my daughter deserve to be shown up for the liars and cheats that you are. So go ahead and report the damages to your precious car. Tell the police I'm the one who caused them. I don't care! I can afford the increased premium on my insurance. But one way or another I'll drive Sally Winslow out of this town, if it's the last thing I do.''

''If anyone should be driven out of town, it's you, for impersonating a pit viper! And not that I owe you any explanations, but I went to Sally's house uninvited. *I'm* the one who got carried away. If it were up to her, she'd be happy never to have to set eyes on me again.''

Colette let out a harsh, ugly laugh. ''Who do you think you're trying to fool? I saw her. She had her tongue halfway down your throat. Another five minutes, and I'd have been treated to the sight of her lying on the floor with her legs spread.''

''I had no idea you were capable of such vulgarity, Mother-in-law,'' he said, coldly furious. ''Did you perhaps learn it from your daughter? I understand she was pretty good at spreading her legs for any man who took her fancy.''

She reared up from her chair, her expression wild. ''You'll be sorry you ever said that, Jake Harrington,'' she shrieked, saliva spraying from her mouth. ''And if I ever hear of you repeating it to another living soul, Sally Winslow isn't the only one I'll run out of town. You'll never again be able to walk down the street again with your head held high, either!''

CHAPTER SEVEN

"PLEASE don't act hastily," Martha Winslow begged, when Sally told her mother about the incident with the intruder and said she was thinking of leaving town as soon as the trial was over. "We're your family and we've seen so little of you since you left university. You've no idea how thrilled your father and I are at the thought of you settling down here at last, and perhaps getting married and having babies who'll live close enough for us to watch them growing up. It means so much to us, Sally."

"I hardly think Margaret and Tom would agree with you. They find me an embarrassment."

Her mother made a face. "Tom's always been a little...conservative. He's more comfortable living by a strict set of rules. That's what makes him such an excellent school principal. But you're different. Margaret knows that and loves you for it. As Tom's wife, though, she's in a difficult position. Her first loyalty is to her husband, and rightly so. But don't assume for a moment that that means she isn't happy you've come home again."

Sally paced to the wide windows in her mother's garden room and looked down the hill to the crescent-shaped bay for which the town was named. At that time of year, with the late winter winds still howling, the surf-capped waves rolled and heaved with furious, restless energy but, under a summer sun, the water turned from glacial green to deep blue, and lapped ashore with leisurely, seductive indolence.

She loved the changing seasons; they were one of the things she'd missed most, living in the tropics. Coconut palms and coral lagoons had their place, but nothing quite compared to beach combing here, after a fierce Atlantic storm, or wading through milk-warm tidal pools in August, with wild blueberries hanging ripe on the bushes just beyond the dunes.

"It's not that I want to go," she said on a sigh, turning to face her mother again. "I really was eager to come home. I just hadn't expected I'd create such a stir practically from the day I set foot in town."

"You've been unlucky and perhaps a little unwise, but all that will blow over in time." Her mother shot her a telling glance. "Frankly I'm surprised you're giving in so easily. I thought you had more backbone than to let some anonymous prankster rob you of your dreams."

"There's more to it than that, Mom. It's Jake, as well."

Her mother leaned forward and stroked her cheek. "You think I don't know that, my darling? You and he share a lot of history and were very close at one time. It's natural that he tugs at your sympathy when he's coping with such grievous loss. He needs plenty of support—but I'm not sure he needs it from you. At least, not yet. Not until all the furore surrounding Penelope's death simmers down. Even then, there might not be any going back to what you once had together. You've changed, and so has he. But there's enough room for both of you in this town. Your life doesn't have to coincide with his."

Her mother wasn't telling her anything she hadn't already told herself. Constantly running away didn't resolve anything. Eventually a woman had to stop and confront her demons. Had to fight for the kind of life she wanted—and she'd wanted so badly to prove that the once-headstrong teenager, more concerned with Jake Harrington than any well-brought-up girl should be, had matured into a steady, responsible woman. She wanted to be accepted into that segment of society she'd once thumbed her nose at.

"I know you're right," she said. "About everything. I

would like to have children and a husband and, yes, a house with a picket fence and roses climbing up the wall. And if all that makes me a cliché, at least I've grown up enough to admit it. But for heaven's sake, Mom, I can't make a career out of snagging a man and dragging him to the altar. I have to have something else to strive for—something that will bring me satisfaction even if I never marry. The problem is, I don't have the first idea what it is I'm looking for.''

''Maybe because you're trying too hard to find it. Sometimes the best ideas come when you least expect them.''

''But I need something to occupy me until then.''

Her mother smiled impishly. ''The annual fund-raising gala's coming up at the end of June, and even though the planning committee's been working on it for months, we can still use all the extra help we can get. The whole affair's grown so much from what it used to be that you'll hardly recognize it. You *will* be attending this year, of course?''

''I don't think so, Mom. I don't have a date.''

''You won't need one. You're going to show up wearing the most gorgeous dress this town's ever seen, and have every eligible man in the county flocking around you, begging for a dance. Not only that, Tom's brother, Francis, is joining our party, and I'm sure he'd be happy to stand in as your official escort for the evening.'' She caught Sally's hands and squeezed them pleadingly. ''Don't disappoint me, Sally. You can spare me one evening, surely?''

Surprisingly, upon consideration, Sally found the whole idea quite appealing. It had been a while since she'd dressed to the nines and sipped champagne from wafer-thin crystal flutes. Life in the Caribbean had tended to be more casual; a sun dress, sandals, and piña coladas in a coconut shell were more the style.

''All right.'' She smiled at her mother, her mood lightening. Maybe she *had* been overreacting by allowing a silly, juvenile prank to derail her plans.

"Just as well," her mother admitted, on a sigh of relief. "I've already bought the tickets and reserved a table for six. Now, about helping out beforehand, we hold the event in the drill hall attached to the old naval training base, these days. The hall itself's not the most glamourous venue, but the gardens around it are lovely, and the officers' club is perfect for predinner drinks, or a quiet place to sit for those who want a break from dancing. Turning the main area into a fairyland is a major headache though. But you're so creative, you'd probably come up with a hundred ideas. If you're willing to volunteer your time and don't mind taking on a challenge, I can keep you busy twelve hours a day for the next month."

"I'll do my best not to let you down," Sally said, wrapping her mind around the idea and finding it, too, rather appealing. "If nothing else, at least no one could fault me for not putting my time to good use."

"On the contrary, the planning committee will welcome you."

"I don't know why."

"Because," her mother said, her eyes misting over suddenly, "regardless of what mistakes you might have made along the way, you're one of us. This is your home. You belong here, Sally."

After a while, Sally actually felt as if she did. Once they got past their initial reservations and realized she was in for the long haul, the other women on the planning committee were thrilled with her ideas for dressing up the stark, unlovely drill hall, and disguising its cold cement floor and bare walls. They approved her sketches, gave her a generous budget to work with, and free rein on how she spent it.

March roared in on an icy blast, but drifted away in a flurry of mild, sun-splashed days. The snow melted and the first crocuses poked their heads above the ground. The incident with the trespasser faded from Sally's memory, along with her bruises.

She appeared at Sid Flanagan's trial and not only managed to avoid Jake who, she'd learned, had also been subpoenaed, but also gave clear and convincing testimony which not only helped convict the accused, but also showed her to be a woman of courage not about to be intimidated by the aggressive cross examination of the defense lawyer.

Suddenly her days were full and rewarding. People smiled acknowledgment when they passed her in the street. A flattering commentary on her volunteer efforts received notice in the newspaper. If Jake himself made no attempt to contact her, other men, including Francis Bailey, Tom's surprisingly nice brother, did. She went out for dinner, to the theater, to house parties.

Then, just when she began to believe her mother had been right and there really was room in town for both of them, she literally ran into Jake one afternoon at a coffee parlor in the Old Mill Arcade, a one-time derelict cavern of a building on the north side of town, which had been turned into a trendy shopping mecca. Like her, he was loaded with purchases, neither was paying attention, and they collided with an almighty bump which sent half her shopping bags flying.

She could hardly pretend she hadn't seen him nor, after he'd recovered her packages and offered to buy her a coffee, could she come up with a plausible reason to refuse. She was too undone by the sight of him.

He wore black cords and a tan leather jacket, a cream shirt and black loafers. The lines around his eyes and mouth were less pronounced. He seemed younger, more rested. Never more attractive, and never more taboo. He threatened everything she'd worked so hard to achieve. He made a mockery of her hard-won independence of him.

When he pulled out a chair for her, she sank into it thankfully, before her legs gave way beneath her. "Espresso," she said, when he asked what she'd like. She needed a jolt of something strong to redeem her from the pitiful weakness attacking her.

"So," he said, frankly appraising her, once they were settled at a table, "you're looking better. No bruises."

"You, too," she replied. "No cane."

He laughed and she wished he hadn't. She didn't need him drawing her attention to his perfect, even teeth. She didn't need to be reminded how talented and versatile his mouth was.

"Not much of a limp left, either," he said. "I guess we're both as good as new, though you carry it off better than I do. You look wonderful in purple—like a crocus in bloom."

"Thank you." She played self-consciously with the single button on the jacket of her linen suit. His gaze followed the movement of her fingers, then traveled slowly up her neck to her face. She felt the color flow into her cheeks and knew he noticed.

Desperate to find some neutral topic, she dragged her avid gaze away from him and brought it to bear on his assorted bags and packages. "You've been shopping, I see."

"A few little extras to make my new place feel like home."

"You've moved?"

If he'd said he'd taken up residence on another planet, she couldn't have sounded more unhinged. Embarrassed, she took a mouthful of her scalding espresso. The pain as it burned its way down her throat made her wish she'd tasted it before she spoke. Maybe then she'd have kept her mouth shut altogether.

"Only to the other side of the hill," he said easily. "I was ready for a change, so I shopped around, found a house I liked, and took possession a couple of weeks back. How about you? Still staying at the guest cottage?"

"For now. I was called to testify against Sid Flanagan, but I dreaded it, and held off making any long-term plans until after the trial. The boy you drove home that night gave evidence, too, against the tavern owner."

"I know."

"You've kept in touch with him?"

"Yes."

How typical! He'd take up with perfect strangers, and ignore her. "Is he staying out of mischief?" she asked lightly.

"Yes. I gave him a job, and he's shaping up well." He paused, and for a second, she thought he was going to elaborate, but he turned the conversation back to the trial. "I'm glad they found enough evidence to put Flanagan away for a good, long time."

"Me, too."

He inspected her again, tilting his head to one side and squinting at her through the fringe of his long, dark eyelashes. "Guess you found it pretty hard, seeing him again?"

She averted her glance and pretended to worry a hangnail. "It was worth it."

"You should think about taking a couple of weeks' vacation, now it's over. Go someplace and soak up a little sun."

With you? she longed to ask, but clamped her mind shut on the unruly impulse and said only, "Even if I wanted to, I couldn't get away. I'm pretty busy with the fund-raising gala."

"So my mother tells me. From all accounts you've injected new life into a pretty tired old concept."

"I'm enjoying the challenge."

She dared to look at him again. The afternoon sun threw long shadows across the coffee parlor and bathed his face in a tawny glow. By what right had he cornered such a lion's share of masculine grace and beauty? she wondered resentfully. Once his period of mourning was over, he'd have every eligible woman under ninety chasing him around the block!

Refusing to give in to the senseless longing overtaking her, she asked, "How are *you* keeping busy when you're not fixing up your new house?"

"I'm taking over the reins of the family business."

The Harrington Corporation was one of the oldest and most prestigious in town, and Duncan Harrington, Jake's father, a force to be reckoned with in the business community. "Your father's retiring?" She shook her head in wonderment. "I can't imagine that."

"He'll stay on as board chairman, but he's kept pretty busy with his duties as mayor and needs someone else to take over the day-to-day running of the business."

"And you feel qualified to do that?"

The question emerged so loaded with venom that she cringed inside, but if he noticed, he gave no indication. He merely leaned back in his chair, hooked one arm over the back and said, "It'll be a learning curve, no doubt about that. But he's always there if I need advice. I'm planning to take the company in a new direction. We've talked things over and he likes my ideas. I'm pretty confident I can handle the job."

"You sound excited about it. I guess that means you've found the long-term challenge you were looking for."

"Yes," he said, and fixed her in another too-penetrating stare. "Have you found yours?"

"Not yet." She pushed aside her coffee cup and pointedly checked her watch. "My goodness, I had no idea it was so late. The arcade will be closing shortly."

"We've got a few more minutes before then."

"You might have, but I'm afraid I don't. I've got a lot of work ahead of me. Thank you for the coffee, and congratulations on your new career."

"I'll walk you to your car."

"No need," she said, collecting her shopping bags and doing her best not to allow the thought that, beside his certainty and sense of purpose, her recent accomplishments seemed little and trite. She *had* to get away from him, before she melted into a pool of unadulterated longing and despair.

He didn't bother to argue. Even less did he accept his dismissal. He simply commandeered half her stuff, gathered up his own, and waited for her to lead the way to her car.

The arcade itself was located in an area of abandoned warehouses. They loomed like dark skeletons all around the parking lot. Figures lurked in the shadows, young people with no apparent place to go, begging for money. It was a desolate scene as the day drew to a close, and Sally was rather glad not to be facing it alone.

They were at her car and she had unlocked the trunk when raised voices attracted their attention. Not far away, a girl, hugely pregnant and with tears running down her face, clung to the arm of a shifty-eyed boy.

"You've got to help me, Billy!" she cried thinly. "It's your kid, too."

"Yeah, *right!*" he sneered, shaking her off so roughly that she staggered. "Mine and who else's? Forget it, loser!"

The utter, wretched defeat on the girl's face and in her posture struck such a chord in Sally that she reacted without thought for the possible consequences to herself. Throwing her bags to the ground, she flew at the boy. "You rotten little creep!" she shrieked. "Don't you dare manhandle her!"

She'd have scratched his eyes out, if she'd had the chance. Yanked out his greasy hair by the roots, one miserable follicle at a time! But Jake's arms came from behind, bodily hauled her off her feet, and slammed her up against the solid wall of his chest with such force that the breath rushed from her lungs in a great *whoosh*.

The boy immediately darted to safety behind the nearest parked car. "Man, keep your rabid bitch on a leash," he yelled at Jake, interspersing every other word with his favorite four-letter obscenity. Then, his source of wisdom apparently exhausted, he took off. The last Sally saw of him, he was bobbing and weaving among the other shoppers returning to their vehicles, until he turned a corner and was lost to sight.

Furious, she thrashed to free herself from Jake's grasp and, in doing so, managed to land him a couple of well-placed elbow jabs to his ribs, which was no less than he deserved. "Why'd you do that?" she spat. "Why didn't you let me deal with him?"

"Because I'm not interested in testifying in another case of assault and battery," he said, calmly brushing himself off.

"He wouldn't have dared!"

"You don't know that. In fact, I begin to wonder if you know much of anything, Sally. Did it ever occur to you that that punk might have had a knife? That you could be lying in this back alley now, bleeding to death from a stab wound?"

"No, it didn't," she raged, "because it seemed to me there was someone else who needed protection more than I did. That poor child over there needed help."

"Which I was more than ready to offer—without starting a street brawl, I might add."

"So offer it now! Do something for her!"

His raised eyebrows spoke volumes of astonishment. "What do you suggest I do, Sally? She's safe enough, at least for now."

"And what about tomorrow, or the day after?"

"I'm afraid there's nothing I can do about that."

"Oh, how very convenient! You'll go out of your way to help a drunk find work, but you won't put yourself out for a girl in trouble. Why am I not surprised?"

"What would you have me do?" he said, almost as angry as she was. "Take her home with me? Adopt her?"

"She's alone and afraid! She needs an advocate."

"Unfortunately she's not alone. There are dozens like her. It's a major problem in this area. Ask my father, if you don't believe me. There's not a council meeting goes by that the subject doesn't come up of what to do about kids living on the street. But there are no quick-fix, easy solutions."

The girl had drawn a shabby sweater over her swollen belly and was pushing an old grocery buggy toward a warehouse close to the railroad tracks at the end of the alley.

"No quick-fix solution for babies having babies?" Sally said scornfully. "Well, there's one I can think of!"

Grabbing her purse, she raced after the girl. "Wait," she panted.

The girl turned, her eyes filled with suspicion, her expression so closed and wary that Sally's heart broke for her. Opening her wallet, she took out all the bills and loose change she had and stuffed them into the girl's hand.

"Take this," she said. "It's not much, but it'll help you buy a hot meal and find a motel room for the night."

When she returned to her car, Jake had picked up all her bags and belongings and stashed them in the trunk. "That was a kind and decent thing to do," he said, slamming down the lid, "but you do realize it's a bandage solution only, and won't fix the bigger problem?"

"Yes, Jake," she said, with heavy sarcasm. "I might be a fool, but that doesn't make me a congenital idiot."

"That's debatable." He opened her car door, helped her into the driver's seat then, before she had time to realize what he was up to, strode around to the passenger door and climbed in next to her.

"I don't recall offering you a ride home," she said.

"I don't recall asking for one."

"Then get out of my car."

"Not until you hear me out."

"I've heard enough already." She started the engine. "And I'm in a hurry."

He reached over and turned it off. "I'm not the one who got that girl pregnant," he said. "In fact, from where I stand, the only thing I did was keep you out of a hell of a lot more trouble than you could handle. That being so, would you mind telling me why it's my head you're ready to rip off? Are you perhaps taking out your frustration on me because your conscience is bothering you?"

"My conscience?" she echoed. "What's my conscience got to do with anything, unless it's the fact that, unlike that poor child out there, I've never known what it's like not to have a red cent to my name?"

"Precisely. You've always had money to buy your way out of any situation which didn't quite meet with your approval."

"And that's relevant now because?"

"Aren't you the one who claimed to want to defend the underdog? Well, here's your chance to put your money where your mouth is. If you really cared about that girl and others like her, you'd do something about it."

"Like what? Open a shelter for troubled teens?"

She tossed out the question with heavy sarcasm, yet even as she spoke, something clicked into place in her mind—as if, after stumbling around in the dark for years, she'd suddenly found a lamp and turned on the switch.

"It was just a thought." Jake shrugged dismissively. "Forget I mentioned it."

But though carelessly conceived, the idea had taken hold with such a wealth of logical certainty that she couldn't ignore it. "I don't want to forget it. You said yourself there are others like her out there, with no one to turn to and nowhere to go. Why not provide them with a safe haven? I *do* have the money. I could afford to take on such a project."

"Are you serious?"

"Yes," she said, marveling. "I absolutely am! Jake, I could make it work, I know I could. All I'd have to do is find suitable premises. Some big old house, with lots of rooms."

"Or a big old monastery that's been standing empty ever since the monks moved to their new digs across the bay."

"Are *you* serious?"

"You bet." His anger forgotten, he let his smile shine in the darkening afternoon like a lone ray of sunshine.

She knew the place he was referring to; a two-story stone building standing well back from the road about five miles east of town, on a slope above the river, with an apple orchard off to one side. "Is it for sale?"

"Has been for over a year, according to my father. It's too big for a private residence, and zoning laws won't allow it to be turned to commercial use."

"I'd need a permit—"

"You need to slow down and think about what's involved, before you go that far," he cautioned her. "You wouldn't just have pregnant girls on your doorstep. There'd be types like her charming boyfriend showing up, too."

"And I'd deal with them. I handled him, didn't I?"

"Yeah," he said, with a grin. "The whites of his eyes were showing and he looked about ready to wet himself!"

This time, she joined in his laughter. "I guess I did get a bit carried away."

"Then maybe you need to slow down and give all this more thought before you make any final decisions. It's easy to get swept up in the heat of the moment, and let's face it…if you do decide to run with the idea, you'd be taking on a huge commitment."

"I've never been afraid of commitment, Jake," she said, her enthusiasm suddenly eclipsed by futile regret.

The parking area was almost deserted by then. Being alone with him in a car, with dusk closing in all around, was altogether too intimate a setting. It stirred up memories best forgotten, of the times they'd driven to some out-of-the-way spot and made love in the back of the Jeep he used to drive. They'd never worried about being discovered. The windows had steamed up too quickly for anyone to see inside—and much the same thing was happening now, albeit for different reasons.

"What?" he said, watching her in the semigloom. "What took the light out of your eyes?"

"Old ghosts," she said, her gaze trapped in his. "And the cold. It's chilly in here now that the sun's gone down."

He leaned over and restarted the engine. "The last is easily rectified. Old ghosts, though…." He shook his head. "They're usually best left undisturbed. Let them go, and look to the future."

"How do I do that, Jake?"

"You chase them away," he said. "Like this."

She wasn't prepared for his kiss, or the surge of desire it inspired, which ran through her like a blowtorch. She wasn't prepared for the low moan of surrender which escaped her throat, or the way every inch of her skin came alive, with each pore opening to welcome him like buds unfurling beneath the seduction of the benevolent April sun.

Her only thought—and not a very coherent one at that— was that nothing would ever appease her hunger for him. Not time, and not another man. Regardless of what career path she might follow, or how rewarding she might find the journey, there would always be a part of her craving only him. The pain of the realization was so acute that she burst into tears.

"Stop hurting me!" she sobbed, tearing her mouth away.

He reared back, his eyes bleak with shock. "Hurt you? My God, Sally, I would never knowingly hurt you!"

Embarrassed by her outburst and the impossibility of trying to explain it, she fought to control it. "You do it all the time," she said, when she could speak again. "Whenever I see you, whenever you leave me, you steal a little bit more of my soul." Her voice sank to a whisper. She pressed a fist between her breasts. "I have to put an end to it. If I don't, I'll have nothing left in here. You'll eventually take all of me."

"And if I tell you I never want to leave you again?" His touch exquisitely tender, he framed her face in his hands and cradled her chin in the hollow formed by his palms. "What then, Sally? Would you let me stay?"

"No," she said, turning her head aside and refusing to allow temptation to get a foothold. "I wouldn't trust your reasons for being there. Apart from anything else, you aren't ready to make such a commitment. You've only been widowed a few months."

His sigh flowed over her, warm and coffee-scented. "Are we back to that again?"

"Yes," she said, staring determinedly through the windshield at the few cars remaining in the parking lot, because to look at him was to invite complete collapse of whatever moral scruples she still possessed. "I can't overlook it, even if you can."

"Would it make any difference if I told you that my marriage had been over for years? That the only reason it lasted as long as it did was the fact that I spent more time away than at home? That even absence had stopped making it bearable?" He cupped her jaw. "Look at me, and listen. If you believe nothing else, believe this—I was going to ask Penelope for a divorce as soon as I was discharged, and she'd have given me one."

"How can you be sure of that?"

"Because she was as miserable as I was." He laughed, a bitter, mocking sound bereft of amusement. "Do you think for a moment that I didn't suspect the kind of life she was leading when my back was turned? Why else do you think I harassed you about the night she died, if not to confirm what I've suspected for years?"

"Whatever Penelope's sins, she didn't deserve to die for them."

"I'm not suggesting she did. But in the end, she was the instrument of her own destruction, and I refuse to be governed by it any longer. It's time to move on, Sally."

He leaned toward her. Pulled her into the circle of his arms. Ran his hand inside the collar of her jacket. Stroked his fingers over her nape so artfully that a prickle of arousal chased down her spine.

"Do you remember how it used to be with us?" he murmured, nudging her mouth with his. "The way we'd never miss a chance to be alone together? How I used to make you laugh, and—?"

She snatched a breath from lungs rendered pitifully inadequate by his seduction. "You don't make me laugh anymore. You frighten me. What's made you so cold and merciless that you can dismiss a young woman's death so easily?"

"I revere life too much ever to dismiss it easily," he said. "That's one of the things war teaches a man. Nor do I hold Penelope solely to blame for the disintegration of our marriage. I was equally at fault."

"*You* cheated on *her?*"

"I didn't sleep with other women, if that's what you're asking. But if marrying her when I knew I didn't love her the way I should have is cheating, then yes. If infidelity of the mind amounts to the same thing as infidelity of the body, then yes again. I cheated on her."

"Why did you marry her, if you didn't love her?"

"Because I let pride come between me and the woman I really wanted. Because I never thought the day would come when I'd again get the chance for this."

His hand stole over her shoulder to the front of her jacket. Deliberately, he undid its solitary button and splayed his fingers over the silk shell she wore underneath.

"I can feel every beat of your heart keeping pace with mine, Sally. It's been so long since I did that."

She willed her breathing to remain even. Forced herself not to betray her body's screaming acknowledgment of his touch. But he mistook her silence for permission, and continued his voyage of rediscovery.

His hand slid lower, scorching over her breasts to her ribs, and past the flat contour of her stomach to the top of her thighs. His mouth scattered fleeting kisses along her jaw, nibbled a path from her ear to the base of her throat and from there, in one smooth sweep, to her nipple. She felt the heat and dampness of his mouth penetrate the thin fabric, and was helpless to prevent the puckering response of her flesh beneath.

"Stop!" she begged, knotting her fingers in his hair and wondering how the stern rebuttal she'd intended somehow emerged as a blessing.

"I will," he said. But he didn't. Instead his hand lingered

a moment at her knee, then trailed under the hem of her skirt and gently pried her legs apart.

Horrified by the abrupt flood of arousal dampening her underwear, she said with a lot more conviction, "Jake, I mean it! We can't do this!"

He leaned his head against the back of the seat, closed his eyes, and let out a mighty sigh. "I know, I know! You're afraid someone might see us. We're not teenagers anymore. You think it's too soon for me to be getting involved with you again. People will talk, and there's been enough speculation already." He expelled another long, frustrated breath. "You name it, I've thought about it. Why else do you think I've stayed away from you, except to spare you becoming the object of public censure and curiosity again? But, Sally, I've missed you. I ache to hold you again. Damn it, I want to let go of the past and start over. With you."

"I want that, too," she cried, the vehemence of his declarations spurring her to admit her true feelings, "but not sneakily, like this. Not fumbling around in some dark parking lot, as if the only thing that matters is sex when we both know there's so much more to a relationship. And not in plain view of the next person with a notion to spy through the window to see how much dirt they can dig up on us."

"You want me to date you? Come calling on a Saturday night, and take you to dinner and the theater? Broadcast to the whole world that we're a couple?" He flung out his hands, palms upturned. "I'm more than willing, if you are."

She shook her head, regret sweeping over her in long, cold waves. "No. Not yet. Not when I know it would create gossip. You might not understand this, but I like being regarded as a good woman, instead of a bad girl."

"Then what *do* you want me to do? Leave you alone for

another six months and pretend you don't exist? I've already tried that, sweetheart, and it doesn't work. Look what happened, the first time we found ourselves alone together.''

''There has to be another way, surely? Some middle ground?''

''A way for us to be together, without anyone being the wiser?'' He sat silently a moment, then slapped the flat of his hand to his forehead. ''There is! Of course there is! I have the perfect answer. Come to my new house.''

Be alone together, with no one and nothing to apply the brakes when passion threatened to run amok? ''Oh, I don't know about that! I can just imagine—''

''Think about it, before you reject the idea out of hand: no pressure, no demands, no conditions, just you and me getting to know one another all over again, at leisure and without any outside interference. Don't we deserve that much?''

Oh, the temptation he offered! But dare she agree? Dare she trust her heart, which heard only the promise in his voice, when her head was warning her that the chance of recapturing their enchanted past was slim at best, and not worth risking her future over?

''No one will ever know,'' he said. ''The house is hidden from the street. There's room for your car in my garage. It can be our secret hideaway, the place we escape to, to make the waiting more bearable.'' He reached for her hand and kissed each finger in potent persuasion. ''Come on, Sally. What do you say?''

CHAPTER EIGHT

SHE drove down the quiet lane just after eight the next night, and never would have suspected a house lay tucked behind the high hedge if he hadn't drawn her a map showing the unpaved driveway winding between a thick stand of maples.

"We'll have dinner," he'd said, "and talk. And if matters progress beyond that, it will be because you choose to let them."

Awash with hope and false confidence, she'd agreed. It had seemed, at the time, a reasonable enough suggestion. They were both mature adults, after all, and understood the principle of mind over matter. Only now, with the beam of her car headlights slicing across the front of a low-slung stone house set in a hollow above the cliffs, did the foolhardiness of the venture strike home.

But it was too late to change her mind. Even as she contemplated throwing the car into reverse gear and beating a fast retreat, the overhead door to the garage rolled up like a huge mouth waiting to swallow her. Caught between exhilaration and despair, she nosed her car into the empty space beside his.

No sooner had she killed the engine than the door rolled down again, and he stepped out of the shadows to welcome her. He squeezed her hands briefly, dropped a kiss on her cheek, and said, "Hi. I'm happy you're here."

Very nice. Very civilized. Very nonthreatening. So why were her legs trembling and her pulse leaping erratically?

"I didn't bring a housewarming gift," she babbled, desperate to fill the void following his remark. "I thought I'd wait to see what kind of decor you've chosen, first. There's nothing worse than having to pretend to like something you'd never have bought for yourself, is there—especially when it comes to knickknacks? They're a very individual, personal choice, don't you think? Some people can't get enough of them, and others can't abide them.''

"What I think,'' he said, drawing her gently through a side door into the house and guiding her down a narrow, softly lit hall, "is that you're afraid you've made a mistake in coming here, and are desperately trying to find an excuse not to stay.''

She attempted a laugh, but managed only a slightly hysterical giggle. "Is it that obvious?''

"Only to someone who knows you as well as I do.'' He stopped before an old-fashioned armoire and unwound the silk and Pashmina shawl from her shoulders. "You don't have to be afraid of me, Sally. I meant what I said yesterday. You set the pace of this, and every other meeting.''

All at once feeling foolish, she said, "Thank you for being so understanding.''

He hung her shawl in the armoire and led the way across a wider hall to a long living room with windows set on each side of a stone-fronted fireplace. The walls were painted white, and a faded, quite beautiful Turkish rug covered most of the dark oak floor.

Two plump armchairs and a three-seater sofa, upholstered in navy corduroy, curved around a glass-topped coffee table in front of the hearth. To one side was a wrought-iron wine rack, topped with a slab of dark green marble on which stood a pewter ice bucket and two tall champagne flutes. Above the mantel hung a painting in the Constable style, of grayhounds against a backdrop of dark, leafy trees. A large antique map in a carved frame graced the wall opposite.

He'd started a fire to banish the chill of the late April

evening. The flames leaped and crackled up the chimney and flung gaudy images over the polished brass andirons. The only other source of light came from several thick white pillar candles set in heavy brass holders placed strategically at various points around the room.

The total effect was so warmly inviting that Sally forgot to be nervous and exclaimed, "You put all this together by yourself?"

"Afraid so," he said, grasping the neck of the bottle chilling in the ice bucket.

"I think you've done a spectacular job!"

"I like it." He hoisted the bottle for her inspection. "Perrier Jouet okay?"

"Always!"

He poured the champagne, and lifted his glass in a toast. "Here's to old friends and new beginnings."

"Yes." She sipped from her glass, aware that although they both might pay lip service to the concept, the atmosphere hummed with a prophetic subtext far exceeding anything as straightforward as friendship. The evening had barely begun, and already she was floundering in the emotional undertow they were both working so hard to ignore.

Deeming it wise to maintain a little distance, she boycotted the chair he indicated and wandered about the room, stopping to admire a writing desk in one corner, and bending to inhale the delicate fragrance of a vase of scarlet and purple anemones on a side-table.

"I remembered they were your favorite flower," he said, watching her.

"Did you?" A wave of pleasure washed over her, sweeping her ever deeper into dangerous waters. "They're lovely, and so is your home."

"It's my kind of house. Unpretentious, solid and built to last."

"Is it very old?"

"About a hundred and fifty years. I'll give you the grand tour later, if you like."

"I'd like," she said, even though she knew it would be safer to decline. "I'd like it very much."

"Does that mean you're not sorry you didn't stand me up, after all?"

"Yes," she said, circling the room again. "I'm very glad I decided to come."

"Enough to relax and enjoy yourself?"

She glanced up sharply and found him leaning against the mantelpiece, his eyes unreadable. "I suppose so, but I wish you'd stop scrutinizing me like that."

"I can't help it. I find you very lovely."

"Actually, we look a bit like twins afraid of color," she said, drumming up a nervous smile at the coincidence of her having worn a long black skirt and ruffled white blouse to complement his black slacks and long-sleeved white shirt.

"I prefer to see us as an unfinished work of art," he replied, without a flicker of amusement. "The sketching's in place, but the harmony of color has yet to be decided. Are you hungry?"

The mere thought of forcing food down her throat almost made her gag. On the other hand, dining solely on champagne promised nothing but trouble she couldn't handle. "I am, rather."

"Good," he said. "So am I. But I'm not planning to eat you alive, Sally, so stop prowling like a caged animal, and come sit by the fire while I take care of a few things in the kitchen."

"May I help?"

He topped up her glass before heading for the door. "Not tonight. Next time, perhaps."

Would there be a next time? *Should* there be?

She was still debating the question fifteen minutes later, when he came back and announced dinner was ready.

"Good heavens!" She paused on the threshold, amazed at the sight before her. "What an unusual room!"

The dining area was circular, with a domed ceiling from which hung a delicate bronze chandelier. Floor to ceiling windows, topped by a painted frieze of exotic birds soaring against a pale blue sky, ran all around the room, except where built-in china cabinets flanked each side of the archway connecting it to the rest of the house.

Two chairs at a round table, centered on a fringed rug of the same shape, echoed the rotary theme. The only other items of furniture were another six chairs following the outer curvature of the floor, three to each side of a long, elegantly simple sideboard stationed on the far side of the room, parallel to the entrance. Candle flames flickered in here, too, but unlike those in the living room, were mirrored over and over in the night-dark glass of the uncurtained windows.

"An eccentric architectural feature," Jake remarked, ushering her forward. "One of many in this house."

"But charming, nonetheless. I love it!" She flung a wary glance at the windows. "At least, I think I do."

"If you're worried about anyone spying on us, don't be. There's nothing out there but ocean and sky. This part of the house sits at the edge of the cliffs. We won't be bothered by Peeping Toms tonight."

"That's a relief!" She took her seat, vividly aware of his presence as he pushed her chair a little closer to the table, then let his hand rest briefly on her shoulder before he assumed his own place across from her. "I'd hate to have an uninvited guest intrude and spoil yet another evening."

And nothing did. It was just the two of them engaged in conversation, with a Chopin nocturne playing softly in the background to absorb any awkward pauses which might arise. The combination of champagne and ambience worked a special magic, aided in no small part by the excellence of the meal. Vichyssoise, followed by lobster Mornay and baby asparagus, was no mean feat for anyone, least of all a man who claimed he knew next to nothing about cooking.

"I ordered it from a restaurant," he confessed, waving aside her compliments. "All I had to do was remember to turn on the oven. Steak on the barbecue is my only forte in the culinary department."

The pièce de résistance, though, and the one thing which reduced her to putty in his hands, was his choice of dessert. Layers of tangy orange mousse and whipped cream sandwiched between feather-light slices of sponge cake and decorated with curls of white chocolate, it had been the specialty of a little French bakery in the Square. They'd discovered it when they first started dating and it had come to symbolize everything that was good about their relationship.

"You remembered this, too," she marveled, overwhelmed.

"I remember everything about that time, Sally."

She sighed. "So do I. We celebrated every special occasion with this cake—our one month anniversary, our first Christmas together, Valentine's Day, our birthdays…" Thoroughly bedazzled, she ventured a glance at him.

"The first time we made love," he said, his blue eyes holding her prisoner. "And the last."

He spoke with such a world of regret that when she replied, her voice was embroidered with tears. "Please don't," she begged. "You said yourself, there's nothing to be gained by raking up old ghosts."

He shrugged assent. "All right. Let's talk about something else. What really triggered your response to that girl, yesterday afternoon, Sally? The fact that she was pregnant?''

''No. The fact that she was just a child and had no one to turn to.''

''If you follow through on your idea to open a shelter, it'll make a huge difference to others like her.''

''But it'll come too late to help her. Her baby must be due any day now, which means there'll be yet another homeless child out there.''

''Is that the only thing that's troubling you?''

''No,'' she said, her spirits dampened by painful memories of herself feeling every bit as afraid and alone, when she'd been of a similar age, and in a similar situation, to that girl.

''But you can't tell me what it is?''

''No. You wouldn't understand.''

''Try me,'' he said. ''You might find you've underestimated me.''

Was that possible? *Could* she learn to trust him enough to share the secret of her pregnancy with him?

''Perhaps, some day,'' she said. ''But not tonight.''

''All right.'' He didn't press the point. Instead, when they'd finished eating, he pushed back his chair and held out his hand. ''Come. We'll have coffee in the other room.''

''Let me help you clear away these dishes first.''

''You just want to check out the kitchen, to see what kind of a slob I really am,'' he teased.

Relieved at the lessening of tension, she laughed and said, ''How'd you guess?''

''You keep forgetting how well I know you.''

If anyone *had* been watching them through the window, they'd have appeared to be a couple enjoying good food, fine wine, and the simple pleasure of each other's company. But it was all an illusion. They might be interacting like

rational adults on the surface, but undercurrents of awareness swirled between them at a deeper level.

They were alone in a cosy, isolated house which carried
no bad associations for either of them; a private secluded
world all their own. And every accidental touch—fingers
touching fingers, as they collected the dishes, shoulder
brushing against shoulder, as they passed each other in the
kitchen—reinforced the fact.

The message, potent as forked lightning leaping from one
sensory point to another, was undeniable. And sooner or
later, she knew they'd have to acknowledge it. Not surprisingly, it caught up with them when, after they'd had
coffee, he took her on the promised tour of the rest of the
house.

Most areas presented no problem. When he showed her
the little atrium off the back of the house, her pleasure was
unfeigned. She sincerely admired the double-pedestal desk
in his office. "Very handsome," she remarked, tracing a
fingertip over its finely tooled, leather-inlaid top. "Do you
plan to do much work from home?"

"Why not? I'm away all day, but I don't have much of
a social life right now, so I'm here most evenings, and
there's still plenty to do with the company reorganization."

She looked at the rolls of blueprints stacked in an old
umbrella stand. "You never did explain what that involved.
Are you expanding the downtown premises?"

"What, and have the entire population of Eastridge Bay
coming down on me for tampering with a heritage building? Not likely!" He cupped her elbow and directed her
across the hall. "You're not far off the mark, though. I'm
planning to revitalize the north end of town. To my mind,
it's as much a part of local history as the Harrington
Building or the Burton Tower."

They were headed for the stairs. Trying hard not to hyperventilate at where they led, she said, "You mean the area we were in yesterday?"

"The very same. Ever since the fish packing company closed down, most of the buildings have fallen into disrepair, which is a shame. Now it's a shanty town for people like that girl we met."

"And you'd like to turn it into a money-maker again."

He threw open the door of the first room off the upper hall, and said reprovingly, "You make 'money' sound like a dirty word, Sally. It doesn't have to be, you know. It can do a lot of good when it's applied to a just cause."

"You call turning people out of the only home they know 'a just cause'?" she retaliated, less because she wanted to argue the point at that moment, than to distract herself from the sight of the big sleigh bed, with all its attendant connotations of intimacy.

"Never mind trying to pick a fight with me," he said, standing back to let her precede him into the room. "Think instead about us making love in here, when you're ready. When you trust me enough to share all of yourself with me."

She'd have told him that trust cut two ways and that once it was broken, it wasn't always possible to repair it. But her train of thought, already sadly impaired, collapsed altogether when she saw the photograph hanging on the wall above the bed.

It was a head shot of herself, taken during their last summer together. She was looking straight into the camera, her eyes wide and candid, her mouth tilted in a half smile.

"Yes," Jake said in a low, smoky voice, from his post at the door. "That's you—back in the days of your innocence."

"I wasn't so innocent," she said shakily. "We'd been lovers for over a year."

"And would be still, if we hadn't let other people come

between us.'' He came up behind and took her by the shoulders. ''How did that happen, Sally?'' he asked, planting a soft, spellbinding kiss on the side of her neck.

Hazy with encroaching pleasure and knowing she was fast losing her grip, she forced herself to say, ''You grew tired of dating a teenager and went looking for someone more sophisticated.''

She heard the hiss of his sharply indrawn breath, felt his grip tighten ominously, and found herself being spun around to face him. ''I did *what?*''

He wore such a look of wounded bewilderment that she almost let it deflect her from the truth. Almost! ''You took up with someone else,'' she said firmly.

''Not so!'' He shook his head, as if to clear away the confusing mists distorting his memory. ''*You're* the one who turned to someone else—the guy in Paris…your French roommate's older brother who appeared late on the scene to show you around the city and introduce you to its night life.''

''Night life—with *Emile?*'' She burst out laughing. ''Whatever gave you the idea there was anything romantic between me and Emile? He was a Roman Catholic priest, for heaven's sake, whose only passions were his religious calling and seventeenth-century French painters! Yes, he showed me around—the different museums. And yes, he introduced me to Nicolas Poussin—who, in case you're wondering, died in 1682!''

The thunderous silence with which Jake greeted that revelation defined his shock louder than a drumroll. He reeled away, paced to the window, braced his hands on either side of the frame, and stared out at the night, his spine rigid as iron.

When he finally whirled back to face her, she quaked inside. His face was white, his eyes dark as midnight, his mouth so compressed that if she hadn't known differently, she'd have thought it incapable of laughter or a smile. "A *priest?*" he repeated, his voice chillingly quiet. "I guess that's something Penelope forgot to mention when she regaled me with your doings."

There was no need to ask what he meant by that. Sally understood immediately, though she wouldn't have, eight years ago. Back then, she'd still thought Penelope was her friend.

His contained embitterment suddenly exploding into wild fury, Jake grabbed a book on the bedside table and flung it across the room. "That witch!" he ground out savagely. "I'd kill her with my bare hands, if she weren't already dead!"

"She's not the one who was to blame," Sally said, the enormity of Penelope's machinations seeming not nearly as reprehensible as their own stupidity. "We are. If we'd trusted each other—"

"Don't you dare make excuses for her!" he bellowed. "Don't you *dare* try to shift the blame to us!"

"Why not? If we'd believed in one another—"

"We were kids, for Pete's sake! Look at that picture hanging over the bed, if you don't believe me. You were the only girl I'd ever been with. I was your first...." He slammed his fist against the wall in impotent rage. "What the hell did we know about anything?"

"Not enough, obviously. If we had, we'd have reacted differently. But we can't go back and change any of it, so we might as well forget it."

"I don't think so, Sally! Not in this instance. Just because something's painful to remember doesn't justify denying it ever happened. You don't learn anything by doing that. You merely leave yourself open to being hurt again in the same way."

"I don't think I could ever be hurt like that again." For all her brave words, her voice broke when she continued,

"When we ran into each other, the Christmas after I came home from France, you were so cold. And that girl you were with…the way you looked at me, the way you flaunted her in my face…you behaved as if you hated me, Jake."

"I certainly tried hard enough to do just that." In three swift strides, he crossed to where she leaned against the bedpost and pulled her so hard against him that the breath flew out of her lungs. "But it didn't work. What you saw wasn't hatred, my lovely, it was anger and hurt pride. And the girl…" He kissed the top of her head, wound his arms around her tighter than ever. "She was just that—a girl, looking for a good time."

"She was so pretty, so animated. I felt nondescript beside her. Pale and uninteresting."

"Oh, honey, never compare yourself unfavorably to her or any other woman! She was fun, but neither of us was ever serious about the other. She was a diversion. A way to help me get over you."

"Were you lovers?" she asked, her throat constricting as she remembered the way the girl had looked at him; the way she herself once had looked at him. With private, intimate knowledge.

He pressed her face to his chest. "What does it matter, after all this time?"

"*Were* you?" she persisted, needing to know.

"Yes," he admitted on a sigh. "For a short while. Until the night I called her Sally, by mistake. Then it was over, for both of us." He held her at arm's length and looked at her searchingly. "I don't have the right to ask you this, but have there been other men for you?"

"No," she said, a tear slipping down her face. "I've wanted there to be. I've tried to make it happen—but at the last moment, I couldn't go through with it. You spoilt me for anyone else."

"Let me make it up to you now," he whispered hoarsely, drawing her down beside him on the bed and stringing a row of kisses across her eyelids and down her cheek to her mouth. "We've wasted so much time, my lovely Sally. Let's not waste any more."

He sounded so sure; so certain they could recapture all that they'd lost, and she wanted desperately to believe him. But there was more to their history than he knew.

How could she, in good conscience, exact information from him, yet keep secret the fact that she'd been pregnant? It had been his baby, too. And although she'd once thought he didn't deserve to be told, she now believed otherwise. He had a right to know the truth.

He might not take the news well. He might become angry and not want her anymore. But if that was so, better to find out before he broke her heart all over again, because such secrets almost always found a way to leak out, sooner or later.

"I don't think we should get carried away like this," she began. "I think we need to talk more. So much has happened—"

"Talk can wait," he muttered, rolling her onto her back and gazing down at her as if he'd never grow tired of the sight of her. "There's only one way to erase all those lost years, and that's for us to become one again. I want to feel you naked beneath me, Sally. I want to look at you—at all of you. I want to fall asleep with you in my arms and wake up beside you in the morning. And most of all, I want to lose myself inside you, again and again, because that's the only way I'll ever be able to forget what a damned fool I've been."

His words, his kisses, drained her of caution—and most important, of the will to resist him. She was putty in his hands. His to do with as he pleased. Whatever he asked of her, she would give.

Ask? That was a laugh! She was his willing slave. He didn't have to ask for a thing. She was his for the taking. She always had been.

Dimly, she was aware of him removing her blouse, her camisole, her bra. His lips blazed a trail over her skin and left behind a galaxy of sensation as dense as a shower of winter-spiked stars.

He touched her in the old familiar way. Rediscovered her with deft, tormenting brushes of his fingers and mouth until the sharp edge of desire sliced at her without mercy, and her flesh screamed for release. Heat, fluid and tempestuous, seared her.

Still, she could not silence the prompting of her conscience, and so she tried again to unburden herself. "You might not want me, if you knew—"

He took her hand and stroked it down his torso until she found that part of him grown so heavy with arousal that not even the barrier of his clothing could hide it. "You think I don't want you, my Sally?" he groaned, his eyes twin flames of blue fire as her hand closed around him instinctively, possessively. "Think again!"

"You don't fight fair," she whispered on a dying sigh, loving the burning strength of him against her palm.

"I fight to win," he replied. "I fight for what I believe in, and I believe in us."

"So did I, once upon a time, but something went wrong, Jake…!"

"Because we made mistakes," he said, "But now we'll make it right again."

She was in thrall to him, so drugged with mindless pleasure, that she was barely aware he'd almost stripped her naked until he slipped his thumb inside her panties and stroked it over the moist, satin fold between her legs. At that, she turned into a tigress, clawing at his shirt, wild to reacquaint herself with the smooth texture of his skin, and the long, strong muscles which had so captivated her before.

He uttered a low growl of triumph. With haphazard disregard, his fine cotton shirt landed on the floor next to her black crepe skirt. Her panties floated through the air, a silken, insubstantial parachute, and came to rest sprawled brazenly atop his briefs.

Then, it was as he'd said it had to be, with the two of them locked in a tight, urgent welding of flesh within flesh, and the race began. She clung to him, willing time to fly backward and let it be as if nothing and no one had never come between them. She gave herself up to the deep, desperate rhythm he imposed. Felt herself teeter achingly close to the brink of total surrender.

"Stay with me, sweetheart," he muttered tensely, his breathing deep and desperate as he battled to resist the completion threatening to overpower him.

She tried. But at the last, she could not. She was too oppressed with guilt. The best she could do was hold him close and mourn a little as he was swept to a place where she could not follow. And she realized that it wasn't the same between them and never would be again.

The tapestry of emotion was more richly textured, the design more intricate. Not a boy-and-girl thing at all, but a man-woman relationship with all the depth and complexity that implied.

They could never go back to the safe, idealistic state they'd known as teenagers. Too much had happened in the interim. Their only choice was to advance into the uncharted territory of an adult relationship, and hope they could evade the pitfalls littering their path.

Eventually, his breathing slowed and he lifted his head to look down at her. "You didn't come," he said, stroking the hair away from her face. "Have I lost my touch, sweet Sally?"

"No," she said miserably. "It was my fault. I was too tense…too preoccupied." Sorely troubled that they could have loved so deeply and still lost so much, she touched his cheek. "Oh, Jake, something happened that last summer we spent together…something I should have told you about at the time and didn't. I thought I could forget it, that it was in the past, but now that we've found each other again, it's preying on my mind. But I'm afraid to tell you in case it spoils…"

He kissed the tears pooling at the corners of her eyes. "Don't be afraid," he said. "There's nothing you can't tell me."

"Oh, but there is." Her voice sank to a whisper, and she clung to him. If she found the courage to confess, and he couldn't forgive her, this would be the last time she'd ever lie in his arms. Wouldn't she be better off learning to live with the burden of silence? Or would it taint this second chance to recapture heaven?

He tipped her face up to his and when she tried to turn away, held her chin between his thumb and forefinger so that she had no choice but to meet his gaze. How uncompromisingly direct his eyes were.

"Look at me, Sally, and stop putting yourself through all this unnecessary grief," he said sternly. "If it's the baby you're worrying about, there's nothing to tell. I already know. I've known about it for years."

CHAPTER NINE

THERE'D never been a more beautiful spring morning. Sunlight splashed on the polished wood floor of his kitchen, the coffeemaker burbled in harmony with the birds perched on the feeder outside the window, and Jake, wearing only blue jeans unsnapped at the waist, mixed champagne and orange juice for mimosas.

"We could make a habit of this," he said, dropping a kiss on the back of her neck. "You could move in and the three of us could live happily ever after."

"The three of us?"

"You, me and this." He tasted the Hollandaise sauce she was preparing for their eggs Benedict and smacked his lips appreciatively. "Don't worry, I was careful last night and used protection. You're not pregnant."

"We were careful before, and I got pregnant anyway."

"Accidents happen sometimes." He stroked her hair. "No point now in beating ourselves up about it."

"I was so afraid you'd be angry when you heard."

"I was, at the time," he said, a shade too grimly for her peace of mind. "Livid, in fact. But I got over it. You were young and afraid."

"How did you find out?"

"I'll give you three guesses, and the first two don't count."

"Penelope, of course." She rolled her eyes. "Why did I even bother to ask?"

"If she'd said something at the time, instead of waiting until after the fact, I've have been there for you. You wouldn't have gone through all that alone. But she didn't, and neither did you, and I see no purpose in belaboring the issue at this late date.''

Again, the hint of something hard and cold in his voice, as difficult to pinpoint as a grain of sand trapped in molasses, cast a shadow over the bright morning. ''But it was our baby, Jake,'' she said softly. ''A little person created purely from love, the way all babies should be made, and I wish so much things could have turned out differently. Perhaps if I'd come to you—''

''But you didn't.'' Abruptly, he swung away and made a big production of checking the sliced ham and English muffins warming in the oven. ''Let it go, Sally. I have.''

''Are you sure? You don't sound like a man—''

''At the risk of repeating myself *ad nauseam,* we can't undo the past,'' he said curtly. ''The best we can do is make damn good and sure we handle things differently in the future, if we ever find ourselves in the same situation again. How are those eggs coming along?''

She didn't want to cloud the morning further by pointing out that, because the pregnancy had been doomed from the start, they couldn't have done things any differently the first time around, either. He was right. She had to move on— and she could, now that her conscience was clear and there were no more secrets between her and Jake. ''They're done,'' she said, drumming up a smile.

To her relief, he responded in kind. ''Then let's eat! A man needs to build up his strength after the kind of workout you gave me last night. By the way, did I mention how fetching you look this morning, Miss Sally?''

''Oh, I don't think so!''

Her hair was still damp from the shower, she was barefoot, and she wore one of his shirts. Hardly the most romantic way to greet the day, or face your lover across the breakfast table. Suddenly self-conscious, she pushed back the sleeves which, although she'd rolled them back, kept slipping down her arms. She wished she'd thought to put on her panties.

"You're blushing," Jake said wickedly. "You really shouldn't stand in the sun like that, my lovely. Everything you're trying so hard to hide is illuminated in perfect detail under that shirt, and it's driving me wild. Maybe we should forget breakfast and move this discussion back to the bedroom."

"After I've slaved over a hot stove to make you breakfast? Not a chance!" She spooned Hollandaise sauce over their eggs and passed the plates to him. "Here, make yourself useful."

He carried their meal to the breakfast nook, took a seat across from her, and clinked the rim of his mimosa glass against hers. "Thank you for last night, Sally. It meant a lot that you stayed."

"To me, too, though I don't know how I'll ever be able to look your mother-in-law in the face again."

It was entirely the wrong thing for her to say. As quickly as his voice had overflowed with warmth and tenderness, it turned cold again. "My mother-in-law doesn't enter into it. She has no bearing on us, and particularly not on you or your doings."

"That's not quite true. She's on the gala committee, and I can't avoid her. We've seen quite a bit of each other in recent weeks."

"I hadn't realized," he said, his surprise evident. "Is she giving you a rough time?"

"Not really. She's softened up quite a bit, probably because I follow orders without argument, generally make myself useful, and otherwise stay out of her way."

"That's Colette, all right. Happiest when she's dishing out commands and having everyone else jump to do her bidding."

"Well, you have to hand it to her, Jake. Whatever other

shortcomings she might have, she's good at organizing people—and keeping busy probably helps her cope with her grief.''

"I guess it beats her other pastime," he said cryptically, "but what's she going to do once this shindig's over?"

"I doubt she's thought of that. I guess, like the rest of us, she's taking things a day at a time. Will you be attending?"

"The gala?" He inspected his mimosa thoughtfully. "I hadn't planned to, but I will if you're going to be there."

"Even though we can't be seen together."

"You mean, we have to pretend we're not on speaking terms?"

She laughed, but it was an effort, because he clearly didn't find anything amusing about the prospect. "We don't have to go quite that far. We can be civil to one another but, for appearances' sake, Tom's brother, Francis, will be my official escort."

His mouth tightened ominously. "And you expect me to meekly go along with that? Fat chance!"

"You have to! It's just to spare both of us unnecessary criticism and gossip. After all, it was only a few months ago—"

"That I buried my wife. I know, and I'm growing tired of hearing about it. I'm sorry Penelope's dead—don't get me wrong about that—but I'm not sorry to be rid of her, and frankly, this whole mourning farce is wearing thin."

"But society expects it."

"Which society?" he exploded, flinging down his knife and fork, and shoving aside his half-finished meal. "Not the one I spent most of the last year in! The people there didn't have the luxury of observing polite niceties, and if I learned anything from them, it's this: life's too precious to be put on hold, and a damn sight too short to be wasted."

"We're not talking about forever, Jake," she said, striving to combat his anger with sweet reason.

"Then for how long? Six months? A year?"

"Somewhere between the two, yes."

"And that's okay with you?" He glowered. "You might be prepared to skulk around that long, but I'm not. I'd rather be up-front about who I'm seeing, and take the flak that comes with it."

"I'm not sure I would," she said, a shade wistfully. "I rather like being accepted. It makes a nice change from being regarded as the town pariah."

"What's it going to take for you to feel you've finally made the grade, Sally? Walking through the streets in sackcloth and ashes, and apologizing for being a normal woman with normal needs?"

"It beats proving I'm no better now than I was when I went slinking around, afraid people might learn I disgraced my family by being single and pregnant."

"You're not the only one who paid dearly for that. A woman's lucky in some respects, if you ask me. There's no way a man's going to show up on her doorstep just when she's got her life back on track, and say, 'Hey, you had a baby no one ever told you about! How about that?'"

"That's a rotten thing to say, and you know it!"

"What I know," he said bitterly, "is that if kow-towing to outside opinion now matters more to you than I do, I have to question how much you really care about our being together again."

"I didn't say I didn't care, so please don't twist my words! Do you think I'd have stayed here last night, or that I'd have made love with you, if I didn't cherish every single thing about us?"

"Don't ask me! I'm beginning to think I don't know the person you've become. You never used to be so hell-bent on pleasing everyone else."

"Just because I choose not to fly in the face of convention all the time doesn't mean I'm not the same person inside. I've learned to choose my battles more wisely, is all."

"You've let this town's tight-ass upper-crust matrons subdue your zest for life."

"Or perhaps I've grown up." Disheartened by yet more evidence of this darker side of him, she tried to bridge the chasm threatening to separate them by reaching for his hand across the table. "Six weeks ago, I never thought I'd wake up to find your leg thrown over my hip and your arm anchoring me next to you in that big bed upstairs. I never thought I could fall into a sleep so sweet that if the future hadn't suddenly turned gloriously full of hope and promise, I'd have been happy never to wake up at all. Does that sound to you like a woman who's lost her zest for living?"

"Not as long as she can keep it a dark, dirty secret."

"Oh, Jake!" She sighed, at a loss. "Look, I understand your frustration at having to wait a decent interval before you can resume a 'normal' life. But the Burtons have lost their only child and regardless of whether or not Penelope brought her death on herself, for us to flaunt our affair openly when they're still in mourning goes beyond adding insult to injury."

"Is that what you call it—an *affair?* Gee, and to think I saw it as a time for responsible, unselfish lovemaking—a time for discovery, for unspoken commitment. Clearly I was wrong."

"That's emotional blackmail," she retorted, shaken, "and I refuse to be a party to it."

"And if I refuse to be a party to deceit?"

"Then I guess we've arrived at a stalemate," she said, her voice wobbling with distress.

"Finally we agree on something!"

Hollandaise sauce didn't sit well on a queasy stomach. Swallowing, she pushed her chair away from the table. "I think this was a mistake, after all."

"*This?*" he said, his voice larded with scorn. "Are we talking about this morning's eggs, Sally, or last night's sex?"

Refusing to give in to the misery threatening to undo her, she said with superb composure, "I'm not the only one who's changed, Jake. You're different, too. I fell in love with a man who was both compassionate and even-tempered, neither of which quality you appear to possess."

"I'm sorry I've disappointed you," he said, sounding anything but. "Clearly pretense sits more easily with you than it does with me."

"It isn't a matter of pretense—!"

He dismissed her objection with a shrug. "It doesn't matter what name you put on it, it still comes down to the same thing for me. Putting on an act in public and pretending we're merely acquaintances is dishonest, whichever way you cut it."

"That's not what you said yesterday. Yesterday, you were all in favor of keeping our liaison under wraps."

"Call it the desperate act of a man who mistakenly thought he had nothing to lose when, in fact, he had nothing to gain but a load of aggravation he doesn't need." He raked a tired hand through his hair. "Sorry, Sally, but I've been living a lie for the last four years, and that's long enough for any man. I can't do it anymore. I won't."

"Then I guess there's nothing more to be said."

"Not a damned thing," he replied, with stunningly hurtful indifference. "If you want to wait until dark before you leave, rather than risk being seen in broad daylight, be my guest, but you'll excuse me, I'm sure, if I don't offer to keep you company?"

"I wouldn't dream of asking you to," she said. "I'll go now, and be happy to do so. There's too much risk in my staying here."

That afternoon, rain swept in from the sea and persisted for a week, beating down with such ferocity that the newly opened daffodils, too defeated to put up a fight, lay with their faces battered into the dirt. Much, Sally reflected, as she wished she could do, every time she allowed herself to think of how easily she'd fallen into bed with Jake and how quickly she'd come to regret it.

Another woman might have taken comfort in the knowledge that, for a few, brief hours, she'd known the wonder of connecting with him again, on every level. After that first, tension-fraught exchange, her inhibitions had fled and she'd responded to him with her old abandon.

There'd been no secrets between them; no issues still unresolved. So much of him had been as she remembered—loving, passionate, strong—that it had been easy to convince herself to ignore the other aspects of his personality which weren't the same.

Some of the time, they'd lain together, touching each other in the old, endearing way. She'd run her hand over the long, lean line of his flank. Kissed the scar disfiguring his thigh. Wept a little for the pain he'd endured. Quaked at the danger to which he'd been exposed, and admired the courage which had driven him to ignore his wound and concentrate only on piloting his damaged aircraft back to its home base.

They'd talked idly, trying to bridge the gap of the years they'd been apart.

"How did Penelope feel about your having kept that photo of me?" she'd asked him, lying with her head on his chest and his arm around her.

"She didn't know," he'd said, walking his fingers down her spine with such exquisite finesse that she'd shivered with delight. "I'd forgotten I still had it. I found it when I started packing up my things to move out of the old house. It was stuffed inside a copy of an old high school year book. You wore your hair longer then. When did you cut it short?"

"When I went to California. I wanted to make a fresh start, with nothing to remind me of what I'd left behind."

He'd wound a strand around his finger. Tugged on it gently. "Did you forget me?"

She rolled onto her back. Feasted on the sensual pleasure of the way their bodies brushed teasingly against one another. "I tried to, but you're not easy to forget."

"Nor you."

And sweetly, trustingly, they'd made love again.

But it had all been a dream; a mirage which had disintegrated in the fresh, clear light of morning. Too soon she'd become vitally aware that she and Jake had been apart much longer than they'd ever been together, and that she'd plowed headlong into intimacy less with a lover she knew well than with a virtual stranger.

The boy had indeed become a man, and in the transition, had acquired a toughness, an impatience and an anger which were foreign to her. Worse still, she'd sensed all this beforehand, yet still she'd allowed him to blunt the finely tuned perimeters of her self-preservation. By giving in to unwise desire, she'd let him slip past her guard to reclaim his place in her heart.

The shame of it all tormented her to the point that she briefly considered running away again. Instead she dug in her heels, hid her misery from those around her, and kept busy with preparations for the gala. But she looked ahead, too, knowing that she needed a more permanent goal to pursue once the event was over.

The idea of opening some kind of youth shelter, which had fermented at the back of her mind for weeks, took on new and urgent life when she heard that Jake Harrington's plans to revamp the warehouse district had reached the point where a dozen homeless teens would soon be turned out on the street. She made inquiries into buying the abandoned monastery across the river, found she could well afford the asking price, and arranged to inspect the property.

The location was ideal: tranquil, pretty, and far-removed from the seamy section of Eastridge Bay which most of the town's well-heeled residents preferred not to recognize. The building itself would require some modification, but the general layout, with many small rooms upstairs and the large kitchen and living areas on the main floor, lent themselves well to her vision.

She spoke to a lawyer and, between them, they came up with a proposal which he presented before council. At the end of May, she received approval to go ahead with her plans and completed the purchase.

She told the family her news at a dinner hosted by her sister and brother-in-law on the Tuesday before the gala.

"We're so proud of you," her father said. "You've always been at your best when you've got something you can really sink your teeth into."

In typical fashion, Margaret saw only the possible drawbacks and pitfalls. "Let's hope you haven't bitten off more than you can chew," she chimed in. "The kind of people you're proposing to take in aren't kicked out of their homes for no good reason. Petty thugs and thieves are what you'll be dealing with more often than not."

Surprisingly Tom didn't share his wife's doubts. "I think she's onto something, Margaret," he said. "I've seen the way she interacts with teenagers. She knows how to handle them."

His brother, Francis jumped into the discussion. "I've

got some useful contacts in the hospitality industry. I'll be glad to put you in touch with them, if you like.''

"I look forward to taking you up on the offer, when the time comes," she said.

"Not nearly as much as I'm looking forward to Saturday night," he told her.

He was such a nice, self-effacing man, with none of the bombast which too often marked Tom's personality, and was very attractive, in his own quiet way. She'd enjoyed getting to know him better, and come to be very fond of him.

Maybe there was life after Jake Harrington, after all, she concluded. And maybe she'd needed one more night with him to find the closure which had eluded her the first time around. It had been an expensive lesson but, in the long run, might turn out to be worth the heartache it had entailed.

She'd been so busy, she never got around to finding something to wear to the gala but, buoyed with rare optimism, she talked her mother into going shopping with her. The next morning, they boarded the early train to the city, a hundred miles down the coast, and spent the day scouting the boutiques for the perfect outfit.

They struck gold almost at once, coming upon a gown newly imported from Europe. Strapless and made of white silk chiffon heavily embroidered with overblown white silk roses, it fell in diaphanous layers to a handkerchief hem which dipped almost to the floor on one side and rose to mid-calf on the other.

"You need shoes," her mother decided, as they celebrated over a lunch of fresh crab washed down with Chardonnay, at a charming seafood bistro on the waterfront. "White peau de soie, with a heel. And jewelry. Great-aunt Miriam's diamond necklace and earrings, perhaps?''

"Just the earrings, I think. As I recall, they're practically the size of robin's eggs. Wearing the necklace as well would be overkill. What are you staring at, Mother?''

"You. I haven't seen you this happy in such a long time. The ghosts have gone from your eyes."

"That's what shopping will do for a woman."

"It's not the shopping that's done it, Sally, and we both know it. You're glowing from the inside out. Is Francis Bailey the reason?"

"No," she said honestly. "It's got more to do with my being at peace within myself. It's been years since I've been able to say that and mean it. I've really come home finally, in more ways than one."

"Will you ever feel able to talk about what it was that made you so eager to escape in the first place? Your father and I always supposed it was because things hadn't worked out between you and Jake, but I've often wondered if there was more to it than that."

"There was." She smoothed her napkin over her lap, wondering how much she dared tell. "We had more than just a simple boy-girl romance, Mom."

"I know. You were lovers."

Astonished, Sally met her mother's gaze and found it full of love and understanding. "How did you know?"

"Even if you hadn't been the talk of the town, I'd have had to be blind not to see the way things were between you. But it didn't end there, did it?"

"No. While I was in Paris, I discovered I was pregnant."

"Oh, my poor baby!" Her mother looked out over the water, and when she turned back, her eyes were glazed with tears. "I wondered at the time if that might be the case. Why didn't you come to me?"

"I miscarried shortly after I came home. There seemed no point in burdening you with something you could do nothing about."

"You must have been devastated."

"I was. And ashamed, too, at having let you down. You'd given me everything a girl could possibly want—love, security, freedom—and look how I repaid you."

"A parent's love doesn't hinge on approval of everything a child does, Sally, and if you thought it did, your father and I didn't do nearly as good a job as you give us credit for."

"You're right. I should have had more faith in you." She gave a little shrug. "But all things considered, things probably turned out for the best. Jake and I weren't right for one another."

"Are you sure?"

"I wasn't, for the longest time, but I am now. It's been eight years, Mom, and time hasn't stood still for either of us. He and I have grown apart. We're set on different paths now."

"He's creating quite a stir in the business community, I'll grant you that. When his father was at the helm, the Harrington Corporation stuck pretty much to the traditions which made it successful in the first place, but things have changed since Duncan handed over the reins to Jake. He's striving with a vengeance to fulfill all his ambitions."

"I'm not surprised. He was always single-minded and never believed in half-measures. With him, it was always a case of all, or nothing." She finished her wine and set down the glass with a delicate but decisive thump. "I'm happy he's discovered an outlet for his energy. I wish him every success and hope he's finding civilian life full and rewarding."

She was able to speak with utter conviction because she truly believed every word she said.

Her ideas for decorating the drill hall translated into a reality which surpassed even her high expectations. Yards of billowing, semisheer fabric the color of cherry blossom, draped the walls and hung in swags from the raftered ceilings. Hundreds of tiny foil stars sprinkled over the imported dance floor glimmered in the light of an enormous antique chandelier rescued from the attic of the oldest residence in town. Banks of gardenias and roses perfumed the air. Pink and white candles glowed on the linen-draped tables.

"You've worked a minor miracle!" people exclaimed.

"Fabulous!" others gushed. "Incredible!"

Even Colette Burton favored her with a nod of approval. "Very nice," she murmured, as she passed by. "And your dress is quite lovely, my dear. You do us all proud."

Overhearing, Francis said, "In case I haven't already made it clear I second that opinion, let me say again that you're easily the most beautiful woman in the room, Sally." He offered her his arm. "Shall we take a tour of the silent auction before we sit down to dinner? I want to make sure no one outbids me on your dance card."

"Tell me you're joking!" she exclaimed, still too flabbergasted by Mrs. Burton's compliments to take him seriously. "The suggestion was tossed around that all the ladies involved in pulling this affair together put themselves on the block to raise more funds, but I didn't think anyone actually followed through on it."

"Come and see for yourself," he said. "Not only has the idea evolved into a reality, it's such a hit that it'll probably become a tradition."

Dazed, she followed him to the officers' club where items donated for auction were arranged on long, velvet-covered tables lined up against the walls. As always, people had given generously. Everything, from heirloom jewelry to modern art, restaurant vouchers to weekend retreats, spa memberships to theater tickets, was offered. And, astonishing though it might be, dance cards printed with the names of every woman who'd given of her time and effort to make the evening a success.

"I see I have competition," Francis said, eyeing hers and scribbling a figure and his signature below the last bid. "Half the men in this town are giving me a run for my money."

But it was the *amount* of money they were willing to spend which left Sally speechless. Although the minimum bid had been set at a modest fifty dollars, the sum had risen to four figures already. Nor was she the only one reeling in the cash. Every other dance card showed similar sums.

"No one in his right mind should pay over two thousand dollars for a five-minute waltz," she blurted out. "This is crazy, Francis!"

"Not when it comes to supporting worthy charitable causes," he reminded her. "And not when the people bidding have deep enough pockets that they can afford it."

"Well…!" Flattered and more than a little relieved that she'd splurged on a new dress, she smoothed her hand over the filmy skirt of her gown. "I'm flabbergasted, to say the least."

"And the evening's only just begun," Francis said, giving her hand a purposeful squeeze. "Who knows what else lies in store?"

She certainly didn't! If she'd had any idea of the next big surprise awaiting her, she'd have sneaked out of the nearest side door and gone home. But by the time she remembered it never paid to become overconfident, it was no more possible to avoid the man observing her from across the room, than it was to ignore the woman hanging on to his arm as if she were afraid to let it go.

Sally could hardly blame her. Jake in white tie and tails was dashing enough to make any woman stop and look twice. But his impact on Sally dealt a blow which ran far deeper than mere appearances could achieve.

It had been almost ten weeks since they'd seen or spoken to each other—time enough, she'd believed, to overcome her distressing tendency to suffer a relapse at the sight of him. Yet one glance into those inscrutable blue eyes and she was floundering in a morass of hopeless yearning, all over again.

"Is everything all right, Sally?" Francis inquired, regarding her solicitously. "You're looking rather pale all of a sudden."

She clenched her fists hard enough to leave nasty little dents where her nails bit into her palms. "I'm perfectly fine."

Of course, she wasn't. She was a mess, and it was all Jake's fault. Why couldn't he have stayed away, and left her delusions of immunity intact?

But wishing he and his lady friend would disappear in a puff of smoke wasn't going to work. Much though she'd have preferred to do otherwise, Sally had no choice but to pin a smile on her face and confront the situation head-on.

CHAPTER TEN

HE'D come prepared, knowing they were bound to run into each other sooner or later, and certain that he'd carry off the occasion with so much flair that she'd drool with regret for having walked out on him.

Cripes, much he knew! The minute he clapped eyes on her, his brain froze and his tongue stuck to the roof of his mouth. *Where did she find that dress and what the devil was holding it up?*

"Hello," she said stiffly, fixing her glance on a spot just beyond his left shoulder. Her mouth—that mouth he'd fantasized about altogether too often since the last time he'd tasted it—was as puckered up as if she'd accidentally swallowed a pint of vinegar, instead of the champagne everyone else was drinking. "How very nice to see you again."

Yeah, right, Sally! About as nice as discovering you've got head lice! Who do you think you're fooling?

"You, too," he replied, his attempt at blithe indifference putrefying into an inarticulate grunt.

Dismissing him with a faintly pitying lift of her elegant brows, she switched her attention to Ursula. "You look familiar. Have we met before?"

"Only about a thousand times," Ursula said. "We went to school together, Sally. Grade nine. I'm Ursula Rushton, though you knew me when I still went under the name Phillips."

"Of course! How silly of me not to remember." She bent a winsome smile on Ursula and fluttered her hand at the man by her side. "Let me introduce you to my very

149

good friend, Francis Bailey. Oh, and this is Jake Harrington, Francis. I went to school with him, as well.''

"I'd say we did a bit more than that," Jake spat, barely able to shake the man's hand, so peeved was he at the way she tacked him on as an inconsequential afterthought. "Once upon a time, Sally considered me a very good... *friend,* too.''

She didn't miss his deliberate hesitation, or the inflection in his voice. The color ran up her face, deepening her skin to warm honey, and just for an instant she looked him directly in the eye. "You're right," she said. "Once upon a time, I did.''

He held her gaze, such a hollow ache gouging his gut that he winced inwardly at the pain of it. "But we move on, don't we, Sally?''

"Indeed we do." She took a deep breath and smiled at the man by her side. "And on that note, I think we should move on, and find the rest of our party, don't you, Francis?''

"Absolutely," he said, his gaze so worshipful on her that Jake just about choked.

She tucked her hand more securely under Bailey's arm and inclined her head at Ursula. "It was lovely talking to you, Ursula. Perhaps we'll see each other again some time. Enjoy your evening.''

"So that's the way things stand," Ursula said, staring after her. "After all these years, you've still got something cooking with Sally Winslow.''

Regret bitter on his tongue, Jake said, "No. That implies a mutuality which no longer exists between us. But old habits die hard, as you already know. Do you care for more champagne?''

"Yes." With a last glance at Sally's departing figure, she handed him her glass. "I need something to wash the taste of envy out of my mouth. No woman has the right to

be so utterly irresistible to men. Did you see the way
Francis looked at her?''

''I saw,'' he said grimly.

''What's she got that I don't have, Jake?''

''I'm not sure,'' he said, putting a different spin on the
question as he watched Bailey place an altogether too-
familiar hand in the small of Sally's back. But before the
evening drew to a close, he intended to find out.

Although the winning bids were kept secret until the band
began its last set for the night, the silent auction closed just
before dinner. In the interval, Sally managed to recover
something of her poise.

It helped that Jake and Ursula, who were sitting four
tables away with the Burtons, left midway through the
meal, after a waiter handed Ursula a slip of paper.

It helped, too, that over the course of the evening, Sally
became reacquainted with a number of other people she'd
known at school. Between catching up on news of who'd
married whom, and dancing just about every dance, some
with Francis and others with men she'd last known as boys,
she found she was enjoying herself after all, and quite able
to put Jake out of her mind.

What turned out to be the biggest hit of the evening
finally took place just before midnight, when the women
whose names were on the dance cards were called up to
the podium to be claimed by their partners.

Sally's card was among the last to be announced. Francis
had kept such a close eye on the competition that, certain
he'd posted the final bid, she paid little attention to the
sudden mild flurry of movement as people stepped aside to
admit someone coming in through a side door. In fact, she
was halfway down the steps to where Francis waited ex-
pectantly, when the emcee stopped her in her tracks by

declaring that the winning bid had gone to Captain Jake Harrington.

"It can't have," she said sharply. "He left hours ago."

The emcee pointed across the room. "But he came back to claim his prize," he informed her, and to her mixed annoyance and trepidation, she saw Jake weaving a path through the crowd, toward her.

"Stop looking as if someone shoved a broom handle up the back of your dress and try to smile, my lovely," he murmured, drawing her down the last two steps, and pulling her firmly into his arms. "They're playing our song."

If she hadn't known that every eye in the room was on them, she'd have ground her heel on his instep and told him to keep his distance. Instead, she was forced to follow as he swept her into the middle of the dance floor and led her in a flawless foxtrot.

"I hope you find this is worth whatever it cost you," she said, in a low, furious voice. "But just for the record, I am not enjoying it one little bit."

"Sure you are," he replied flatly. "You're wallowing in every second of it and probably hoping I'll try to sneak a look down the front of your dress. But that would be a bit pointless, wouldn't it, considering I already know exactly what's holding up that delectable froth of strapless silk?"

"Don't be vulgar!"

"Vulgar? That's not a very friendly thing to say." He made an unexpected reverse turn which brought her up against his chest so snugly that she could feel the buttons of his shirt pressing against her skin. "And we were once such good friends, weren't we, Sally?"

By then so discombobulated she could hardly think straight, she said, "We could be still, if you weren't so wrapped up in your own wants that you never give a thought to anyone else's."

"That's not true," he countered mildly. "I've followed

the progress of your latest venture with a great deal of interest.''

''Meaning?''

''Meaning I'm very proud of you for sticking to your guns about helping out kids who've never known the kind of privilege or luxury to which you and I were born.''

''Well, someone has to step in on their behalf and from everything I hear, it's not going to be you. Couldn't you at least wait until I have my place up and running before you turf them out of your precious warehouses?''

''It's for their own protection. At present, half those buildings are potential death traps. Not that I'm able to impress that message on the kids in question. As fast as I board up access in one area, they find a way to get in somewhere else, and that, my dear, keeps me awake at night even more than thoughts of you do.'' He indulged in a bit more sudden fancy footwork which had her clinging to him for dear life. ''So you see, Sally, I'm not entirely self-obsessed.''

''I didn't mean to imply that you were.''

The band changed tempo and segued into something slow and dreamy. The lights on the big antique chandelier dimmed to near-nothing. The floor grew crowded as more couples joined in the dancing.

Absently, as if he wasn't really aware of what he was doing, Jake slid his hand up the low back of her dress to caress her skin. ''Didn't you?'' he said. ''I must have misunderstood.''

Determined not to betray the shameful flood of awareness he excited, she said, ''You're doing this out of spite, aren't you?''

''I'm not sure I know what you mean.''

''Sure you do! The only reason you're putting the moves on me in full view of everyone in this room is to feed your own ego.''

"You think so, do you?"

"Yes," she hissed. "You knew very well that I wanted to dance with Francis, but you just can't stand to lose out to another man."

He dropped his arm. Released her hand. Stepped away from her. "If that's what you believe, then go to him. If he's who you really want, I won't try to stop you."

She fought the truth, but it wouldn't be silenced. "He...isn't," she admitted, her voice sinking to a defeated whimper.

"Then I feel sorry for the poor sod. He's so far gone on you that he'd donate both his kidneys to keep you happy, if you asked him to."

"Whereas you cared for me so little that you couldn't wait to replace me with someone else."

He caught her in his arms again. "If you're referring to Ursula, I'm merely the understudy for the man she hoped would be her escort tonight. She and her husband split up recently."

"Because of you?"

"No, Sally," he said soberly. "Because of another woman. Contrary to what you might choose to believe, I revere the sanctity of marriage and have never chased another man's wife—or cheated on my own. But nor am I averse to lending a friendly shoulder to lean on, once in a while."

"So why did Ursula leave early tonight, then? Did you have a falling-out?"

His voice quivering with devilish laughter, he said again, "No, my lovely. You're the only woman who makes a career out of picking fights with me. She was called home because one of her children became ill."

"I'm sorry. I hope it was nothing serious."

"A case of too many strawberries for dessert, I understand. Why don't we change the subject and talk about us?"

"What's the point? There is no 'us.' You made that clear enough, the last time we were together."

"Because temper got the better of me. I tried to see things your way, Sally, but feelings I thought I could control rose to the surface and took me by surprise. I told myself they were wrong. Indecent. Unforgivable. But the only indecency lay in ignoring them, the only thing unforgivable, lying to myself and you."

She was so mesmerized by his words that she hardly noticed he'd waltzed her out of the drill hall and into the gardens, until her heels sank into the lawn and caused her to miss a step. At that, a flutter of alarm winged its way up her spine. "Why have you brought me out here?"

"Because I'm going to kiss you, and I didn't think you'd appreciate having everyone watch me do it."

She swatted feebly at his hands as they came up to cup her face. "I don't want you to kiss me," she said.

His mouth grazed hers. "Why do you even bother telling such lies when neither of us believes you?"

Oh, he was arrogant—bold—dangerous! So sure all he had to do was exert a little charm, and she'd forget how coldly he'd sent her packing before, and fall eagerly into his arms again.

Injecting considerably more starch into her voice, she said, "*I* believe me. I find I'm quite liking life without you."

"Are you?" he said, undeterred, and ran the tip of his tongue lightly over her lower lip. "I quite detest mine without you."

"What you detest, Jake," she said, warming to the subject, "is not getting your own way. You detest that I didn't come running back, begging for yet another chance to make things work between us. You detest that I wouldn't settle for an illicit affair. For being your mistress in secret.''

He slid his hands down her arms, sank his fingers into the filmy clouds of fabric clinging to her hips, and jerked her close. ''Tell me you haven't missed this,'' he said, his voice suddenly raw and his meaning unmistakable. ''Dare to tell me again that you haven't missed *us*.''

And just that swiftly, the warmth of her indignation turned to searing, sensual heat. She sagged against him, every pore, every nerve ending, reaching out to absorb him. She lifted her face, parted her lips on a sigh, and let him in.

At first, it was enough. To be in his arms again, to indulge in the magic he wove with his mouth, with his tongue, to hear the muttered endearments he couldn't contain—they sufficed. For a little while. But just as puffs of cloud could billow and boil without warning into a storm, so a deeper hunger, a stronger need, suddenly roared to life.

With a muffled growl of frustration, Jake tore his mouth free. ''This is too damned public, even for me,'' he muttered, glaring at the open door of the nearby drill hall. And before she had time to anticipate his next move, he grabbed her wrist and dragged her down the sloping lawn to where a trellis, heavy with wisteria blossoms, offered a screen of privacy.

She should have been outraged; should have resisted. Instead, she surrendered. Exulted in the bruising strength of his grip, in the harsh, impatient rasp of his breathing. And quivered all over with shameless anticipation for what she knew would happen next.

The grass was velvet soft, perfumed with early summer, dotted with tiny daisies. ''I don't want to hurt your dress,'' he said, pulling her down beside him and plucking impatiently at the delicate fabric. ''I don't want to hurt you. But Sally, I need you so badly, I'm afraid I'll do both.''

"The dress doesn't matter," she whispered, and closed her mind to the voice of caution warning her that his other misgiving posed a far greater risk.

"You shouldn't have worn it. All this skin...." He groaned and bent his head to nip gently at her bare shoulder. "Did you do it on purpose, Sally, to torment me? Did you choose it because it showed only a glimpse of one leg when you move, and you knew I'd go crazy wanting to see more?"

"Yes," she said, the ugly truth vaulting out of nowhere to slam her into startled awareness. "I wanted you to notice me."

Less gently, he tugged at the strapless bodice. The silk resisted briefly, then slithered down to expose her breasts. "Did you want me to do this, as well?" he rumbled, his mouth plucking at her nipples and stirring them into electrifying sensitivity.

"I wanted you!" she cried, in an agony of despair. "Everything I do, everything that I am, *always* comes back to my wanting you! But I didn't think you felt the same. You sent me away...you were so angry with me."

"I know," he said, raising his head to cover her face with butterfly-light kisses. "And I'm sorry. I tried telling myself that you were young and afraid and it was as much my fault as yours. If I'd known, if *you'd* known you could count on me, everything would have been different and you wouldn't have cared about what other people thought. We let each other down then, but when you still refused to be seen with me after we'd finally found each other again... hell, Sally, I couldn't take it a second time."

Had he drunk too much wine, she wondered, confused by the disjointed context of his words, or were they simply talking at cross purposes? Uncertain, and knowing only that she couldn't bear the river of pain flowing through his voice, she said, "All I've ever wanted is to be with you, Jake."

"Then come back to the house with me," he urged, adding persuasion to his plea by running his fingers under her skirt to caress her thigh and press the heel of his hand against the passion-dampened swath of satin between her legs. "Let me love you all night long."

The potent intimacy of his touch left her so beside herself with longing that she'd have gone with him in a flash, had a burst of laughter from the other side of the trellis not brought her to her senses as bracingly as a pail of cold water splashed in her face.

What was she thinking of, to be rolling around on the ground, within hearing and seeing range of the hundreds of people who, only a short time before, had applauded her? Why was she leaving herself wide-open to criticism and censure, after she'd worked so hard to redeem her reputation?

Horrified, she pushed his hand aside and clamped her legs together. "I can't!"

"Why not?" The question hung in the air, smoky with passion.

"Because," she said, scrambling to her feet, "it wouldn't be the right thing to do."

He lay spread-eagled on the grass and closed his eyes. "Oh, for Pete's sake, are we back to that again?"

"Yes," she said, hardening her heart against the weariness she heard in his voice. "Anyone could find us here, including the man who's supposed to be my escort."

"Perhaps it would be a good thing if he did. It'd spare him getting ideas of his own about where his relationship with you is headed."

"It would be shameful, and I refuse to subject him to that kind of humiliation."

"What you're really saying, then, is that he comes first."

"Don't make this about him, when it's really about me. It might not seem important in your eyes, Jake, but I like being respectable—and respected. I like being able to look Mrs. Burton in the eye without blushing, and knowing she no longer regards me with such hostility."

"That's because Fletcher made her read both the police and the autopsy report on Penelope, and she can't hide her head in the sand any longer. She's seen irrefutable proof of the kind of life her daughter was leading behind everyone's back, and realizes she can't go on blaming you for the accident."

"I don't care what made her change her mind. It's enough that she did."

"Very decent of you, Sally, I'm sure." He bounded to his feet in one lithe leap and brushed his hands over his jacket. "Tell me, is there any room at all for me in this rosy little picture?"

"Only if we can arrive at some sort of compromise."

"Compromise? Pity that didn't enter into your thinking when you decided to get rid of my child. If it had, my son or daughter would be turning eight pretty soon, and we wouldn't be having this conversation."

Sure she couldn't have understood correctly, she stared at him. "What did you say?"

"You heard."

"You're accusing me of...*aborting* our baby?" She could barely bring herself to utter the words, let alone give them any credence. "Is *that* what you were rambling on about, a few minutes ago?"

"You didn't think Penelope settled for telling me only half the story, did you, when it gave her so much pleasure to relate every last disgusting detail, right down to her having to nurse you back to health because you didn't want your family to know you'd visited a back-street abortionist in another town?"

"But it's not true!" she gasped.

"What, that you weren't pregnant? Too late, Sally! You already admitted you were."

"I miscarried through no fault of my own."

"Sure you did," he sneered.

"Ahh!" She pressed both hands to her mouth, cut to the quick by his unadorned cynicism. "And to think I was ready to trust you yet again with my heart! To think I was fool enough to believe that your feelings for me were strong enough to overcome any obstacle!"

"Yeah," he said bitterly. "And to think I was, too."

"Check the records at St. Mary's Hospital in Redford, if you don't believe me. They don't lie."

He must have heard the incontestable ring of truth in her voice because, for a second or two, he stared at her in silence, his gaze so intense, it almost drilled holes through her skull. Then, mouthing an obscenity of self-loathing which made her flinch, he swung away and looked out at the glimmering lights of the boats anchored in the harbor.

The silence following his outburst was hard enough to bear, but when a selection from *Les Miserables* drifted out of the drill hall, beginning with the hauntingly beautiful "I Dreamed A Dream," it epitomized the entire spectrum of their history so poignantly that her heart broke.

His voice floated on the still air, in melancholy counterpoint to the music. "I took you to see this show, the year I graduated from high school."

"I remember."

"You cried all the way through."

"Yes."

"Are you crying now?"

"Yes."

Another second ticked by, and then another, before he spoke again. "Why can't things ever be easy for us, Sally?"

"Because we care too much," she sobbed.

"Do we? Or is it that we never manage to care quite enough to trust each other completely?"

A terrible hopelessness took hold of her then. It would always be like this for them: the potent, simmering sexuality that never slept; the frantic, mindless greed which always gained the upper hand. And, sadly, the regret which always followed.

She looked down at her dress; at the pretty handkerchief hem, soiled now, and at the delicate silk embroidery stained with grass. It was ruined. Just like them.

"You're right," she said. "We never did."

"Will we ever learn?"

"I don't think so."

"So where do we go from here?"

"Nowhere," she said. "The merry-go-round's stopped, Jake. It's time to get off."

CHAPTER ELEVEN

"No," HE said. "I refuse to give up on us. I won't let Penelope win."

But the only reply was the sound of her walking away, her footsteps falling soft and light across the dew-damp lawn.

It took every ounce of grit he possessed not to go after her, but what little sense he still had told him this was not the time. Not while they were both reeling from shock and pain and grief.

Grief…God, how often had he experienced it over the last year, and when was it going to stop? Children mutilated and orphaned by war. Hospitals blown sky-high. Refugee camps crowded with the sick and the dying. A buddy whose jet didn't come back. Another who went home with both legs missing. And a girl he'd loved all his life, and whose heart he'd crushed under his heel, because he was such a damned fool that he'd listened to the one woman he'd known for years he couldn't trust.

The lights across the harbor misted over and he blinked furiously, not because grown men didn't cry—he knew that wasn't true; he'd seen them with their faces buried in their hands and their shoulders heaving, and heard the primeval sobs tearing them apart as they mourned a fallen comrade—but because he didn't deserve the cleansing release of tears. He deserved the big, ugly chunk of frozen misery lodged in his throat and clogging his airway.

Looking up, he saw the sky was covered with a shimmer of stars. Was she looking at them, too, and thinking of him? Was she still crying? Was Bailey lending her his handkerchief and holding her? Perhaps telling her he loved her and, if she'd let him, he'd make sure no one ever made her unhappy again? Would he, Jake, one day pick up the morning paper and find a wedding announcement on the social page: *Mr. and Mrs. Byron Winslow are pleased to announce the forthcoming marriage of their youngest daughter, Sally Elizabeth, to Francis Bailey, who deserves her a hell of a lot more than Jake Harrington ever did?*

Oh, no, not that! Not as long as he had breath in his body! "It isn't over," he told the quiet night. "Not by a long chalk. I don't care if it takes another eight years, I'll win her back, one way or another."

Keep busy. She didn't know who'd first dished out such advice, but it was the lifeline to which Sally clung in the days following, and it saved her sanity. She threw herself into the renovations needed on the monastery and if nothing quite managed to ease the persistent ache in her heart, at least she found some comfort in the support she received, as word of her endeavors spread throughout the county.

The redevelopment permits she required were issued promptly. The various municipal inspectors who came to assess the repairs and upgrades needed, were helpful, directing her to the most competent electricians, plumbers, stone masons and carpenters in the area.

Francis carried through on his promise. As a result, a discount outlet in the next town offered her fifteen new mattresses and bed frames; another, dishes, cutlery and cooking utensils. A restaurant going out of business sold her stainless steel commercial-quality kitchen appliances at a fraction of what it would have cost her to buy them new.

Friends and strangers alike donated furniture, clothing, linens, pillows, books, television sets. A local nursery promised to prune the neglected fruit trees and clean up the gardens.

A couple in their fifties, the husband a social worker used to dealing with troubled teens, the wife a nurse, applied to be resident house parents.

Sally had begun with a seed of an idea, generated by a chance meeting with a pregnant girl who had no home, and although it remained unalterably *her* project, as the weeks passed and the momentum grew, so did community involvement. And she welcomed it. What mattered was not who was in charge, but that there would be a safe house staffed with caring adults, to which teenagers living on the streets of Eastridge Bay could turn.

What she would not do, however, was accept help from the Harrington Corporation, even though a truck arrived one day with a load of bricks she sorely needed to repave the courtyard at the front of the building. "Take them back," she instructed the dumbstruck driver who could clearly see the ruined state of the area in question. "I don't want them."

A week later, another truck showed up, this time with enough imported Italian tiles to cover the kitchen and laundry room floors. "No, thanks," she said. "I'll shop somewhere else."

Most of all, she refused to take Jake's phone calls. She couldn't. She'd had enough. The pain that came from knowing him just wasn't worth it. They'd crossed a line, the night he'd accused her of aborting their child, and this time there'd be no going back.

It wasn't just the things they'd said to one another in the heat of the moment, which defeated her. It was the much deeper hurt of his having entertained, even for a moment, the idea that she'd willfully destroy the life of his, or anyone else's, child. How did they go about healing such a mortal wound? How could they repair the damage to the very foundations of their relationship?

Francis remained a pillar of support during those difficult

weeks. He never pushed for too much, the way Jake had. He never issued ultimatums.

"I would tell you I love you," he said, one day when he'd persuaded her to take the afternoon off and go for a picnic with him along the river. "But I don't think you want to hear the words, at least not from me."

She could have wept for both of them. He was kind, perceptive, steady, loyal, handsome—all the things any woman could ask for in a mate, and more. Why weren't they enough to make her love him back?

"I wish that weren't true," she said sadly. "I wish it could be otherwise."

"But that's not how it works. We don't choose love, it chooses us. So there's nothing to be gained by lying about your feelings because, in the end, you just end up punishing yourself. Better to settle for nothing, than try to make do with second best."

"But I don't want to lose your friendship. It means the world to me."

He took her hand and pressed a kiss to her palm. "It's yours for however long you want it."

August arrived, and with it, a rash of complications no one had anticipated. The tail end of a hurricane sweeping up the coast brought gale-force winds lasting nearly three days, and dumped over two inches of rain in the region.

Before the storm passed inland, it brought down a hundred-year-old copper beech, causing major damage to the back wing of the monastery and breaking the main sewer line running in from the road. In another area, the roof had sprung a huge leak. Three of the upstairs rooms suffered substantial water damage as a result.

Mice found a way into the cellar and from there, up the inside walls into the attic. In the evening, when the workmen had left and the place was quiet, Sally could hear the scurrying patter of little feet racing between the rafters. Within a very short time, she discovered evidence of them in the big walk-in pantry which she'd already stocked with staples like flour and cereal. Everything had to be thrown out.

She'd hoped to have the shelter ready for occupancy by the end of the month, but she was forced to postpone the official opening until the problems were fixed. They took longer than expected.

One day toward the end of the month, as she was sorting through the mail in the room she'd set aside as an office, she heard a vehicle draw up in front of the house. Expecting it was yet one more tradesman come to work on the repairs, she paid no attention until, several minutes later, she heard footsteps pause in the hall outside the room. She looked up to find Jake standing in the open doorway, watching her.

The shock of seeing him was so acute, she could barely function. The letter opener slipped out of her hand and landed on the floor with a clunk.

She tried to reach down for it, and couldn't. Couldn't stand. Couldn't run. Her body seized up—except for her heart. It staggered and leaped so erratically, she thought she was on the verge of cardiac arrest.

Finally, she managed to croak, "You're trespassing."

"So sue me," he said, stepping across the room and leaning over her as she sat frozen behind her desk.

"You think I won't?"

"I think you can do anything you set your mind to. But you're not Superwoman, and right now, you've got trouble. What I can't figure out is why you'll accept all kinds of help from total strangers, but you won't let me or my workers get a foot in your door."

"Your foot is altogether too far in my door right now, Jake, and I'd appreciate it if you'd remove it."

He straightened and shoved his hands in the back pockets

of his blue jeans—hardly what she'd have expected the new CEO of the Harrington Corporation to wear to work. She doubted his father would ever have appeared in public in anything but a custom-tailored business suit, silk tie and starched shirt. The way Jake was dressed though, he might have been a lowly company employee so far down on the totem pole that he didn't merit notice, even if he did come blessed with the looks and self-assurance to leave most women panting in his wake.

Most! she reminded herself sternly. She would not become one of them. Not again.

"You know, Sally," he said conversationally, strolling around the office as if he owned it, and inspecting the blueprints tacked on the wall, "I credited you with more brains than this. Which matters more: that you get this operation up and running with all due speed, or that you keep punishing me for my many past and grievous sins?"

"What makes you think I can't do both at the same time?"

"You're cutting off your nose to spite your face."

"But it's my nose, and my face."

He looked at her long and thoughtfully. "Maybe so," he finally said. "But I love them where nature intended they should be. I love you."

"No, you don't!" she cried, the emotions she'd struggled to contain boiling up to the surface again. "A man doesn't harbor unfounded anger and resentment against the woman he loves. He doesn't believe her capable of aborting his child just because someone tells him she did. He goes to her and asks for the truth, confident that he can believe whatever she tells him."

"We were young and naive, Sally. We both made mistakes. You could just as easily have come to me."

"Fine! Then we're even. Consider the score settled and go away."

"I'm sorry you're taking things this way. I hoped you'd see my offer to help for what it really is—an attempt to put things right between us."

"Oh, please!" Strength flooding back into her body, she hauled herself out of the chair. "You think I don't know why you really came here today? You don't give a rap about whether or not I've got problems. The only reason you want to help me get this place finished is so that you can be rid of all those pesky young people presently cluttering up your precious warehouse."

He took another turn about the room. Stopped in front of the window. And finally spun back to face her. "What do I have to do to prove myself worthy of another chance, Sally?" he asked bitterly. "Throw myself off the nearest cliff?"

"You can burn in hell, for all I care," she said, steadfastly refusing to admit how badly she wanted to believe one more chance might be enough to mend what was broken between them.

"I already am, my lovely." He stretched out his hand. Traced his fingers across her cheek, over her mouth, and down her throat. "For me, hell is life without you."

His touch was light, fleeting, but it left behind such an uproar of sensation that her skin puckered from the impact. He stood close enough that she could have counted every long, silky lash framing those unforgettable blue eyes. Every breath she took left her filled with the essence of him...clean, virile. Every inch of him was so powerfully attractive that it took every ounce of willpower she possessed not to fall into his arms.

But although submitting to temptation now might be easier on both of them in the short run, it would be so much more painful in the end. She knew because that was the pattern they'd established. Ecstatic highs followed by soul-destroying lows.

So she pushed him away and said firmly, "Don't! It's over between us, Jake. It has been for a long time. We just weren't smart enough to read the signs."

"I'll never accept that."

"I already have. Please don't make this any harder than it has to be. Please, just go away."

"Tell me you don't love me," he said, hypnotizing her with his low, compelling voice and the burning intensity in his eyes, "and I will."

She took another breath, and drew on her dwindling self-possession. "I don't love you."

He stared at her a moment longer, watching for a crack in her defenses—as if, by the sheer force of his will, he could make her change her mind.

She held his gaze. The tension flowed around them, filling the room to bursting with a high, silent scream.

"I hope you don't live to regret saying that, Sally," he said at last.

And then he turned and left her.

When a man couldn't stand to be alone with his thoughts, or bear to look down the road to see what tomorrow held, there was only one remedy, and that was to drive himself to such a point of exhaustion that, come night, he fell into bed practically comatose. Which probably explained why, by the middle of September, at 2:32 in the morning, it took Jake a while to realize the din which had woken him came not from the alarm on his clock radio, but from the phone standing next to it.

"'Lo?" he muttered groggily, raking a hand through his hair.

It was the police. One of his warehouses was on fire. They thought he'd want to know.

The days were bad, but the nights were worse. She'd come home worn out, make something quick and easy for dinner, and be so tired by nine o'clock that she'd climb into bed and be asleep within minutes. Then, around one, she'd wake up, her mind alive with thoughts of Jake, and that would be it until four, sometimes five the next morning, when she'd finally fall asleep again.

It was a ruinous pattern which Sally seemed unable to break. Finally, those bleak, dark, empty hours became such hell to endure that, to get through them, she took to watching a local television channel which ran old movies throughout the night.

They did the trick. Within an hour, her eyelids grew heavy. Sometimes, she made it back to bed. Others, she fell asleep on the couch in the living room, and awoke at sunrise, chilled and sore from lying too long with her neck at an awkward angle, to hear the TV set blasting out the morning news. It wasn't an ideal situation, but it beat insomnia.

One night, in the middle of September, just two days before the shelter opened, she was debating whether or not she had the energy to turn off the set and stagger upstairs, when the flickering, slightly fuzzy black and white movie abruptly disappeared from the screen and was replaced by live coverage of a reporter speaking into a hand-held microphone.

The scene behind him was chaotic. Fire trucks, police cars and ambulances littered the area. Flames licked over the roof of the building in the background. People ran madly in all directions, or huddled together in horrified groups. Sirens split the night, distorting the reporter's words.

She didn't need to hear what he was saying, though, to interpret his message. She recognized the location, and what was happening spoke for itself. One of Harrington Corporation's recently acquired warehouses was going up in smoke. She recognized, too, both the man to the left of the screen, and the girl he held pinned in his arms and was doing his best to comfort.

And Sally knew, with preternatural foreboding, why the girl—no longer pregnant—was so distraught, and why the man looked over at the burning building with such despair. And a horror like nothing she'd ever known before filled her.

She had no memory of how she came to be in her car, or how long it took her to speed across town along streets mercifully deserted at that hour. She didn't care that when she arrived on the fringe of the warehouse district, she had to abandon her vehicle two blocks away and run the remaining distance in her slippered feet.

She knew only a terrible, suffocating sense of urgency— and dread of what she'd discover when she finally reached her destination.

She found the girl at once. The poor child, on the verge of hysterical collapse, was being tended to by a paramedic.

"Her name's Lisa," an ambulance driver told Sally. He jerked his head at the burning building. "She and a bunch of other kids have been living in there for months. Seems they made a fire to keep warm through the night, but set it too close to a pile of dry lumber. They woke to find the place full of smoke and got out just in time. Trouble is, she's got a baby, a little boy, only a few months old. In the confusion, she thought her friend had taken him. Bottom line, though, is the poor little tyke's still in there somewhere."

It was as Sally had feared. "But someone's gone in to find him, surely? They're not just standing around doing nothing?"

She learned then that, bad as things were, they could get worse. "Oh, someone's gone in, all right. The damn fool who owns the place bulldozed his way past the barricade and went charging in."

"You mean Jake Harrington?" Her voice sounded thin and foreign to her ears. "And no one tried to stop him?"

"Nobody could. He was like a wild animal gone mad." The driver shook his head. "As if our guys don't have enough to deal with already, without having to go searching for him, as well."

She let out an involuntary wail of anguish.

The man eyed her sympathetically. "You don't look so hot, all of a sudden. Is he someone you know?"

"He's someone I know," she managed to say, and clutched at the air as she felt her knees buckle beneath her.

"Whoa!" He caught her before she hit the ground. "You'd better sit in the ambulance with the mother, while we wait for news."

"No. I have to be there when he comes out," she whispered, her eyes searching for that familiar, beloved face…and finding only strangers and the awful, hot, red glow of fire. Yet all she felt was a bitter, penetrating cold which started deep within her and spread until she was shaking all over from it.

"Look at you," the driver chided. "You're not dressed for a night like this. You're not even wearing proper shoes."

His concern was genuine, but she shut him out. Trapped in a nightmare of her own making, she heard only the specter of her own voice coming back to haunt her again. It echoed repeatedly through the empty cavern of her mind.

You can burn in hell, for all I care…burn in hell…!

CHAPTER TWELVE

SHE found a blanket. Draped it around herself and the over-wrought girl. They clung together, two strangers caught up by chance in the same bottomless pit of despair, both of them praying aloud for a miracle to save the life of a lost baby and the man who'd risked his to find it.

Time was measured in heartbeats; a race which never ended but ran in endless circles, driven by the tormenting refrain of all the things Sally had said to him. Untrue things, intended only to hurt.

You just want to be rid of all those pesky teenagers cluttering up your precious warehouse...consider the score settled...go away...it's over between us....

And the worst lie of all, I don't love you!

"I didn't mean it, Jake," she whispered. "I'll love you forever. Please come back so that I can tell you...show you..."

But the memory of how he'd looked when last they'd confronted each other, tormented her. His words filled her with a dread which went beyond fear for his physical safety.

For me, hell is life without you, he'd told her and, at the time, she'd dismissed it as just another ploy designed to worm his way back into her good graces.

Now, though, it assumed a different, deadlier context. He was a brave man. He'd faced danger and bodily injury before without flinching. But if his will to survive was extinguished, what then?

A shout went up from the crowd. Afraid to see why,

173

afraid not to, she slipped her arm around the girl and half-dragged her out of the ambulance to where the driver stood.

"They've brought someone out of the building," he said.

Someone?

Frantic to find out more, she'd have rushed forward if he hadn't prevented it. "You'll only be in the way," he said. "Stand back and let the experts do their job. We'll find out soon enough how things stand."

"Is it my baby?" Lisa asked piteously. "Did they find my little boy?"

"I hope so, darling," Sally said. But although she craned her neck and strained her eyes trying to make out what was happening, all she could determine was a paramedic racing toward the ambulance. Only as he drew close enough for her to hear a baby crying did she realize he carried a small bundle in his arms.

He climbed into the ambulance, wrapped the child in an insulated blanket and slipped an oxygen mask over the tiny face. "You're lucky," he informed the sobbing mother. "He seems to be in pretty good shape. No burns, just a couple of minor scrapes and bruises. Being on the floor probably spared him from the worst—less danger of smoke inhalation down low—but we'll have him checked out in Emergency to be sure. Hop aboard, honey. We're going for a ride."

Aware of Sally hovering anxiously to the rear, the driver asked, "Shall we wait for the guy who went in after her?"

"Uh-uh." The paramedic shook his head and reached back to close the door. "There's no hurry on him. The rest of the team can handle it."

At that, the world tilted and no matter how hard she flailed her arms, Sally couldn't retain her balance. The stars fell in a shower of tiny sparks, and blurred with the receding tail lights of the ambulance. She hit the ground with a thump which knocked the breath out of her.

There's nothing to be gained by lying about your feelings, Francis had said. *The person you end up punishing is yourself.*

He was right about so many things, but he'd failed to mention that, in punishing herself, she'd ended up hurting the person she loved most in the world. Why hadn't he thought to tell her that, too?

A grubby hand swam into her line of vision, and she looked up to find a boy bending over her. One of those who'd been living in the warehouse, probably. He was no more than fifteen and behind the tough facade with which he confronted an uncaring world, she saw the face of a frightened child. "You okay, lady?" he asked.

"No," she said. "I'll never be okay again."

He was used to dishing out orders, not taking them, and if they didn't quit poking at him and shoving him around, he was going to punch somebody's lights out.

"I don't need a hospital," he wheezed, swatting aside the mask they kept trying to put on his face, and sending it flying. "Go play Florence Nightingale to somebody else. God knows, there are enough kids around here who could use a bit of care and attention."

The one in charge stood back and tucked his stethoscope into his pocket. "They're often like this," he said, full of his own importance. Cripes, put a man in a uniform, and he thought he ruled the world! "Strap him down, if you have to, and ship him off. He's inhaled a fair bit of smoke."

"Much you know," Jake tried to bellow, but wound up coughing too hard to make himself clear.

"Take it easy, buddy," wannabe Dr. Know-It-All advised him. "The kids all got out of there in one piece. The only real casualty is your warehouse. It's had the biscuit."

Damn good thing, too! First chance he got, he'd have

the whole lot of them burned to the ground. Some things weren't worth saving.

And others, not worth fighting, he decided, as they finished trussing him up like a Thanksgiving turkey and rolled him toward the waiting ambulance. Sick to death of the sight and sound of everyone and everything, he conceded defeat and closed his eyes. Let them do their worst. He was past caring.

He smelled her before he heard her. Came swimming up out of the most restful sleep he'd known in weeks, and recognized her scent, despite the lingering taste of smoke distorting his senses. Diva had been her favorite perfume for as long as he could remember. She'd been wearing it the last time he'd taken her to bed. She'd worn it the day she kicked him out of her life for good.

Why was she here now? Surely there was nothing left to be said?

Her voice tremulous, she murmured, "Jake, can you hear me?"

Oh yeah! And he'd have told her so if he thought she was going to say anything he wanted to hear.

"Open your eyes, Jake," she begged, and wrapped his hand in both of hers.

He could feel her, too, and that was good. That was very good. He'd known too many men who'd woken up in a hospital bed, unable to feel a damn thing because bits of them had been blown off in combat, or hacked off by a military surgeon.

"There's such a lot I have to tell you," she went on, and she must have leaned on the side of the Gurney, or whatever it was they had him laid out on, because it shifted slightly to one side under her weight.

He thought again about replying but decided it was safer to play possum.

"Jake...?" A sob threatened, but she swallowed it on a long, indrawn breath. He could imagine how she looked at that moment, fighting to control her trembling mouth. Glaring defiantly through a haze of tears.

"*Damn you,* Jake!" The words shot out like bullets...*ping, ping, ping!* "Open your eyes and look at me! I love you, do you hear? I believe in us. *Us!* Don't you *dare* deprive me of the chance to prove it." She punctuated the order with a thump on his shoulder. She actually hit him while he lay on his sick bed, the little weasel! *"Don't you dare!"*

Slowly he lifted his lids. Focused on the ceiling fixture from which a pleasantly dim light shone, and the pale green curtain surrounding him on three sides. Rolled his eyeballs to the right until she swam into view.

"Oh, you're awake!" Although she stuffed her fist to her mouth to smother a spate of giggles, her voice swam with tears. "And you look drunk as a skunk!"

He wet his lips and blinked. "And you look ridiculous," he said, trying to lighten the atmosphere. "What's that thing you've got on?"

She pulled self-consciously on the faded hospital gown she wore over a short pink nightshirt printed with purple frogs which most definitely was *not* hospital issue. "I didn't take time to dress. When I heard about the fire, I just came running to find you." She stroked his hair. "You remember there was a fire, don't you? At the warehouse?"

"Yeah," he said. "And I found the baby. I might be all kinds of a fool in your eyes, Sally, but I'm not mentally defective!"

"You did more than find the baby, Jake." Her hand drifted down his face, rasped over the day-old stubble of beard on his jaw. "You saved his life."

"That's good, isn't it?"

"Of course it is! It's the best news possible."

"So how come you're looking so tragic?"

"Because the paramedics said there was no hurry to get you to the hospital." Her mouth quivered all over again. "I thought they meant you were dead."

"And you're ticked off that I'm not?"

"I'm ticked off with myself," she said, losing the battle with the tears. They splashed down her face in rivers. "I lied to you and to myself, and almost left it too late to put things right."

At that, he gave up. He'd have liked to play the tough guy a bit longer, as payback for what she'd put him through, but the tears undid him. Too many had been shed already. It was time they came to an end.

"I haven't been completely honest with you, either," he said. "I heard everything you said when you thought I was still out cold. And just in case you spoke out of guilt, I want you to know I won't hold you to any of it. We all say and do things we don't really mean when we're under stress."

"But I did mean them," she said. "With all my heart. And if you had died last night without hearing them, I would have died with you. You are my life. You always have been."

He caught her hands and never wanted to let them go. "Do me a favor," he said. "Go find my clothes and somebody to discharge me from this joint. We're getting out of here before I make a spectacle of myself."

"I'll do no such thing," she scolded. "You need rest."

"I need you."

"You have me."

"Then prove it and go find my clothes. We have some serious making-up to do, and it's not going to happen here."

"Are you sure you're up to it?"

He tried to look serious, but his mouth twitched and gave

him away. "Take a peek under this sheet, my lovely Sally, and find out for yourself how very much I'm up to it."

It was enough to persuade her, but it took quite a bit more to convince the uniforms. When they realized he'd leave the hospital anyway, they grudgingly gave him his walking papers and a load of advice he had no intention of following.

Within the hour, he was in the passenger seat of her car and feasting his eyes on her as she drove him home. She still wore the tacky hospital gown over her nightshirt, and fluffy white slippers a lot the worse for wear.

She didn't have a speck of makeup on her face, nor a single piece of jewelry anywhere. A far cry from the vision she'd presented at the gala. Yet every male hormone he possessed was screaming for release and urging him to have at her with all due speed.

Her skin smelled of Diva body lotion, she looked luscious as the golden pears hanging on the tree in his garden, and he'd never found her more lovely or more desirable.

The sun was just peeping over the horizon as she pulled into his driveway. "You want to park in the garage?" he asked her.

"No," she said, turning to look at him from eyes as deep and mysterious as priceless jade. "My priorities have shifted. It no longer matters if anyone sees me here."

He leaned over and with exemplary restraint, kissed her cheek. "I've waited months to hear you say that, Sally, but now that you have, it's been worth every minute of it."

She held his hand and followed him into the house. "Are you hungry? Shall I make you breakfast?"

"Oh, yeah!" he said, pulling her at last into his arms, where she'd always belonged and inching her toward the stairs. "I'm hungry all right—but not for breakfast."

*   *   *

They began with a shower. A long, hot, lovely melding of skin against skin, and big, fat soapy sponges to chase away the bleak, terrifying reminders of the night just past. She scrubbed his back; he shampooed her hair. She flattened her hands over the strong, beautiful contours of his chest. He cupped her bottom. Pressed her against him.

"I love you," he said, against her mouth.

A current of joy ran through her. "I've missed you saying that to me," she sighed.

"If I promise to spend the next fifty years making up for it, will you marry me?"

She burst into tears. It seemed to be the thing she did the most often, lately. "Yes," she said. "Oh, yes!"

He wrapped her in a big, fluffy towel, draped another around his waist, and carried her to his bed. The September sun washed over the tumbled sheets and filled the room with mellow light.

"I don't have champagne or roses," he said, lowering her to the mattress. "I don't have a ring or violins. I don't even have fresh sheets on the bed. They'll have to wait until another time when I'm better prepared. Right now, my love, the only thing I have to give you is me."

"You're all I need or want," she said dreamily, opening her arms to him. "My only regret is that I almost had to lose you forever to realize how precious what we share is."

He came to her in a rush of urgency and heat that melted the chilly isolation which had reigned so long in her heart. He came to her with passion and tenderness and love. In a union of mind and body and soul, he restored her to a tempestuous joy of living she hadn't known in years.

Afterward, with the aching hunger sated for a while, they lay quietly together. The blood no longer raced through her veins, but flowed with a sweet and heavy harmony. Here at last was the bliss which had been missing in their previous encounters: the mutual aftermath of *making* love which promised a tomorrow of *being* loved.

She turned to him, her eyes drowsy with passion. "We made another baby, Jake," she said softly. "I'd swear my life on it."

"I wouldn't be surprised," he said, pulling her to rest against his heart. "But this time, we'll do it right."

EPILOGUE

SHE called the shelter The Haven, and although the formal ribbon-cutting ceremony with Mayor Harrington and the town dignitaries didn't take place until the end of October, Sally opened the doors five days after the fire.

Lisa and her son, David, were the first residents and, by the end of that week, five more girls and two boys, ranging in age from fourteen to seventeen, had joined them. The monastery, which had stood silent and empty for so long, was suddenly filled with the clatter of feet and the cautious laughter of young people who, until then, hadn't known much in the way of happiness or acceptance.

One crisp, frosty morning shortly before the official opening, a farmer from down the road brought over a cart full of the biggest, fattest, most brilliantly orange pumpkins imaginable. "For the kids," he said. "Bet they can't remember the last time they had a real Halloween."

He gave them two black Labrador-cross puppies, as well, "because a house ain't a home without a dog or two in it. And I'll have kittens for you, come the spring. That'll put an end to the mice in your attic."

By sunset, some of the teens had carved enough jack-o'-lanterns for one to glow from every window, and the rest to line the front steps and the driveway. Under the guidance of the housemother, those who didn't want to carve filled the house with the scent of roasted pumpkin seeds, and pumpkin soup, and spiced pumpkin loaves.

Just before dinner that night, one of the girls, a fragile, tentative waif of fifteen, set aside the biggest jack-o'-lantern, plunked Lisa's baby in it so that his sweet little face poked out of the top, and borrowed Sally's Polaroid camera to take a photo. Meanwhile, the puppies chewed up a pair of shoes, and left little calling cards on the living room carpet.

Nobody was upset. Things like that happened. It was what being a family was all about.

In between watching her project blossom into a success beyond anything she'd ever hoped for, Sally tried to keep her breakfast down—because she'd been right; she and Jake had made a baby—and planned her Christmas wedding.

"Don't sew up the side seams of that dress until the last minute," her mother ordered the seamstress making the bridal gown. "We want to be sure she'll fit in it."

"Really, Sally, you and Jake took long enough to sort yourselves out," Margaret scolded, dusting off the heirloom cradle their great-grandfather had made. "Couldn't you have held out a bit longer, and waited until you had a ring on your finger before you got pregnant?"

"I have a ring," Sally said serenely, flashing her diamond. "And it's beautiful."

"It's certainly big enough—and considering you're not even three months along yet, so are you. Are you sure you're expecting only one baby?"

Just after Thanksgiving, she found out that she was carrying two.

"How'd you feel about asking Colette and Fletcher to be godparents?" Jake asked, when he'd recovered from the shock. "It's the closest they'll ever come to having grandchildren of their own, and I'm all they've got left of family."

Considering how wholeheartedly the Burtons had accepted her engagement to their son-in-law, Sally was happy to agree. But then, she was happy about everything, these days. How could she not be, with the tangled uncertainty of her previous life finally straightened out, the future shining with promise; and the man she adored chafing at the bit to make her his wife?

"This is cruel and unusual treatment for a man in my condition," he moaned, when he had to kiss her good-night at the door and spend the night alone at his own house.

But he had no other choice. "There'll be none of that!" her parents decreed, the day he proposed and suggested they set up house together before the wedding. "You're moving back home until you're decently married."

They became husband and wife by candlelight, in an evening ceremony, on December the fifteenth, in the biggest church in town, because just about everyone within a twenty mile radius wanted to be there to wish them well.

It snowed the entire week before the wedding. Eastridge Bay always had snow in December. On the big day itself, though, the clouds scattered and left the sky studded with icy stars, which was as it should be: a perfect night on which to begin a marriage which promised to be as close to perfect as anything to be found this side of heaven.

The world's bestselling romance series.

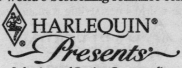

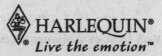

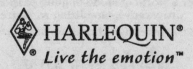

The world's bestselling romance series.

HARLEQUIN®
Presents
Seduction and Passion Guaranteed!

THEPRINCESSBRIDES
For duty, for money...for passion!

Discover a thrilling new trilogy from a rising star of Harlequin Presents®, Jane Porter!

Meet the Royals...

Chantal, Nicolette and Joelle are members of the blue-blooded Ducasse family. Step inside their sophisticated and glamorous world and watch as these beautiful princesses find they have to marry three international playboys—for duty, for money... and definitely for passion!

Don't miss

THE SULTAN'S BOUGHT BRIDE (#2418)
September 2004

THE GREEK'S ROYAL MISTRESS (#2424)
October 2004

THE ITALIAN'S VIRGIN PRINCESS (#2430)
November 2004

Pick up a Harlequin Presents® novel and you will enter a world of spine-tingling passion and provocative, tantalizing romance!

Available wherever Harlequin books are sold.

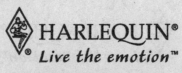

HARLEQUIN®
Live the emotion™

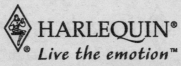

Harlequin Romance®

*What happens when you suddenly discover your
happy twosome is about to be turned into a...family?*

Do you panic? • Do you laugh? • Do you cry?

Or...do you get married?

The answer is all of the above—and plenty more!

**Share the laughter and the tears as these unsuspecting
couples are plunged into parenthood! Whether it's a baby
on the way, or the creation of a brand-new instant family,
these men and women have no choice but to be**

READY FOR BABY

When parenthood takes you by surprise!

**Don't miss
The Baby Proposal #3808
by international bestselling author
Rebecca Winters
coming next month in
Harlequin Romance® books!**

Wonderfully unique every time,
Rebecca Winters will take you on an
emotional roller coaster! Her powerful
stories will enthral your senses and
leave you on a romantic high!

Available wherever Harlequin books are sold.

HARLEQUIN®
Live the emotion™

www.eHarlequin.com

HRBPRW

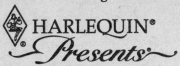

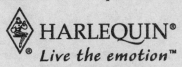